SCIENTIFIC AMERICAN EXPLORES BIG IDEAS

Reproductive Rights

The Editors of *Scientific American*

SCIENTIFIC AMERICAN EDUCATIONAL PUBLISHING

New York

Published in 2024 by Scientific American Educational Publishing
in association with **The Rosen Publishing Group**
2544 Clinton Street, Buffalo NY 14224

Contains material from Scientific American®, a division of Springer Nature America, Inc., reprinted by permission, as well as original material from The Rosen Publishing Group®.

First Edition

Scientific American
Lisa Pallatroni: Project Editor

Rosen Publishing
David Kuchta: Compiling Editor
Michael Moy: Senior Graphic Designer

Cataloging-in-Publication Data

Names: Scientific American, Inc.
Title: Reproductive rights / edited by the Scientific American Editors.
Description: New York : Scientific American Educational Publishing, 2024. | Series: Scientific American explores big ideas | Includes glossary and index.
Identifiers: ISBN 9781725349391 (pbk.) | ISBN 9781725349407 (library bound)| ISBN 9781725349414 (ebook)
Subjects: LCSH: Reproductive rights. | Human reproduction–Law and legislation. | Birth control–Law and legislation. | Women's rights.
Classification: LCC HQ766.R477 2024 | DDC 323.3'4–dc23

Manufactured in the United States of America
Websites listed were live at the time of publication.

Cover: ludovicabastianini/Shutterstock.com

CPSIA Compliance Information: Batch # SACS24.
For Further Information contact Rosen Publishing at 1-800-237-9932.

CONTENTS

INTRODUCTION

On June 24, 2022, the U.S. Supreme Court issued its unprecedented decision in *Dobbs v. Jackson Women's Health Organization*, upending nearly 50 years of reproductive rights in America. The *Dobbs* decision overturned a previous court's landmark *Roe v. Wade* decision of 1973, which ruled that the U.S. Constitution gave women the right to an abortion. The earlier court's *Roe* decision was based on the right to privacy guaranteed by the Fourteenth Amendment to the Constitution.

Since *Roe*, few topics divide Americans more than what legal scholar Laurence Tribe has called this "clash of absolutes." Yet reproductive rights extends beyond issues of abortion to the right to contraception, based on another landmark Supreme Court, *Griswold v. Connecticut*, which in 1965 affirmed married couples' right to buy and use contraception. Battles over reproduction extend to the teaching of sex education in schools, equal access to maternal health care, and other matters. The articles in this collection address all these issues. Some were written before the U.S. Supreme Court's *Dobbs* decision, some in the months leading up to that decision, and some have been written since *Dobbs*.

Section 1, "Historical Perspectives," takes a surprising look back at how abortion and contraception have been treated in earlier periods. Section 2, "Sex Education and Privacy," discusses the concerns about privacy and access to reproductive information. Section 3, "Abortion and Contraception," distinguishes between two medical practices in an age when they are increasingly blurred. Section 4, "Reproductive Science," looks at the role science plays in reproduction. Section 5, "Policy and Politics," brings us into the political world of abortion debates and their implications for government policy. Section 6, "*Roe* v. *Dobbs*," looks at the impact of the Supreme Court's overturning of abortion rights. And Section 7, "Points of View," discusses the overlap between questions of morality and questions of science in debates about abortion.

Section 1: Historical Perspectives

Lessons from Before Abortion Was Legal

By Rachel Benson Gold and Megan K. Donovan

When she went before the U.S. Supreme Court for the first time in 1971, the 26-year-old Sarah Weddington became the youngest attorney to successfully argue a case before the nine justices–a distinction she still holds today.

Weddington was the attorney for Norma McCorvey, the pseudonymous "Jane Roe" of the 1973 *Roe v. Wade* decision that recognized the constitutional right to abortion–one of the most notable decisions ever handed down by the justices.

Weddington understood the ordeal many women faced when obtaining a clandestine procedure, although she kept that knowledge secret for decades. As she has subsequently written and talked about extensively, in 1967 Weddington (née Ragle) became pregnant when she was working three jobs and attending law school.

Without recourse to legal abortion in Texas, she and her partner drove from Austin across the border to a small building at the end of a series of dirt alleys in the town of Piedras Negras. Although Weddington was able to return to Austin and resume law school shortly after obtaining an abortion, the experience wiped out her meager savings. Many other women have told similar stories of pre-*Roe* abortions they, or someone they knew, experienced. For some women, especially those who were too poor, too young, or otherwise unable to find a source of safe care, the clandestine procedure resulted in serious injury or even death.

The pre-*Roe* era is more than just a passing entry in the history books. More than 40 years after *Roe v. Wade*, antiabortion politicians at the state level have succeeded in re-creating a national landscape in which access to abortion depends on where a woman lives and the resources available to her. From 2011 to 2016 state governments enacted a stunning 338 abortion restrictions, and the onslaught continues with more than 50 new restrictions so far this year. At the federal level, the Trump administration and congressional leaders are openly hostile to abortion rights and access to reproductive health care more generally. This antagonism is currently reflected in an agenda that seeks to eliminate insurance coverage of abortion and roll back public funding for family-planning services nationwide.

Restrictions that make it more difficult for women to get an abortion infringe on their health and legal rights. But they do nothing to reduce unintended pregnancy, the main reason a woman seeks an abortion. As the pre-*Roe* era demonstrates, women will still seek the necessary means to end a pregnancy. Cutting off access to abortion care has a far greater impact on the options available and the type of care a woman receives than it does on whether or not she ends a pregnancy.

The history of abortion underscores the reality that the procedure has always been with us, whether or not it was against the law. At the nation's founding, abortion was generally permitted by states under common law. It only started becoming criminalized in the mid-1800s, although by 1900 almost every state had enacted a law declaring most abortions to be criminal offenses.

Yet despite what was on the books, abortion remained common because there were few effective ways to prevent unwanted pregnancies. Well into the 1960s, laws restricted or prohibited outright the sale and advertising of contraceptives, making it impossible for many women to obtain–or even know about–effective birth control. In the 1950s and 1960s between 200,000 and 1.2 million women underwent illegal abortions each year in the U.S., many in unsafe conditions. According to one estimate, extrapolating data from North Carolina to the nation as a whole, 699,000 illegal abortions occurred in the U.S. during 1955, and 829,000 illegal procedures were performed in 1967.

A stark indication of the risk in seeking abortion in the pre-*Roe* era was the death toll. As late as 1965, illegal abortion accounted for an estimated 17 percent of all officially reported pregnancy-related deaths–a total of about 200 in just that year. The actual number may have been much higher, but many deaths were officially attributed to other causes, perhaps to protect women and their families. (In contrast, four deaths resulted from complications of legally induced abortion in 2012 of a total of about 1 million procedures.)

The burden of injuries and deaths from unsafe abortion did not fall equally on everyone in the pre-*Roe* era. Because abortion was legal under certain circumstances in some states, women of means were often able to navigate the system and obtain a legal abortion with help from their private physician. Between 1951 and 1962, 88 percent of legal abortions performed in New York City were for patients of private physicians rather than for women accessing public health services.

In contrast, many poor women and women of color had to go outside the system, often under dangerous and deadly circumstances. Low-income women in New York in the 1960s were more likely than affluent ones to be admitted to hospitals for complications following an illegal procedure. In a study of low-income women in New York from the same period, one in 10 said they had tried to terminate a pregnancy illegally.

State and federal laws were slow to catch up to this reality. It was only in 1967 that Colorado became the first state to reform its abortion law, permitting the procedure on grounds that included danger to the pregnant woman's life or health. By 1972, 13 states had similar statutes, and an additional four, including New York, had repealed their antiabortion laws completely. Then came *Roe v. Wade* in 1973—and the accompanying *Doe v. Bolton* decision—both of which affirmed abortion as a constitutional right.

The 2016 Supreme Court decision in *Whole Woman's Health v. Hellerstedt* reaffirmed a woman's constitutional right to abortion. But the future of *Roe* is under threat as a result of President Donald Trump's commitment to appointing justices to the Supreme Court who he says will eventually overturn *Roe*. Should that happen, 19 states already have laws on the books that could be used to restrict the legal status of abortion, and experts at the Center for Reproductive Rights estimate that the right to abortion could be at risk in as many as 33 states and the District of Columbia.

To be sure, abortion and the after care a woman receives have changed dramatically since the pre-*Roe* era. The alternatives outside a traditional medical setting now available to women involve safer methods, including the use of drugs such as misoprostol for ending a pregnancy. Even so, the truth remains that restricting or banning abortion will not make it go away. These actions will perpetuate inequality because poor women and women of color are more likely than white or wealthy peers to be denied access to care and face legal penalties for seeking alternatives.

In light of state and federal policy makers' hostility to abortion, a commonsense policy goal would be to provide all women access to quality, affordable contraceptive care. In addition to respecting women's human rights and yielding significant health, social, and economic benefits, this step would also lead to fewer unintended pregnancies. In 2014 the U.S. abortion rate reached its lowest level ever recorded, and strong evidence suggests that the steep drop in abortion between 2008 and 2014 was driven largely by improved contraceptive use. Notably, these declines happened in almost all 50 states, including those such as California and New York that are broadly supportive of abortion rights.

Good policy follows where the evidence leads. But the Trump administration and congressional leaders are moving in the opposite direction by pursuing plans that would undermine women's ability to obtain the contraceptive care they need. These attacks include attempts to roll back the many gains of the Affordable Care Act, gut Medicaid, and undercut the critically important Title X national family-planning program, even while attacking Planned Parenthood, a trusted provider of contraceptive services for millions.

Instead of repeating the mistakes of the past, we need to protect and build on gains already made. Serious injury and death from abortion are rare today, but glaring injustices still exist. Stark racial, ethnic and income disparities persist in sexual and reproductive health outcomes. As of 2011, the unintended pregnancy rate among poor women was five times that of women with higher incomes, and the rate for Black women was more than double that for whites. Abortion restrictions–including the discriminatory Hyde Amendment, which prohibits the use of federal dollars to cover abortion care for women insured through Medicaid–fall disproportionately on poor women and women of color.

These realities are indefensible from a moral and a public health standpoint. The time has come for sexual and reproductive health care to be a right for all, not a privilege for those who can afford it.

Referenced

Lessons from Before Roe: Will Past Be Prologue? Rachel Benson Gold in *Guttmacher Policy Review*, Vol. 6, No. 1, pages 8–11; March 2003.

U.S. Abortion Rate Reaches Record Low amidst Looming Onslaught against Reproductive Health and Rights. Joerg Dreweke in *Guttmacher Policy Review*, Vol. 20, pages 15–19; 2017.

About the Authors

Rachel Benson Gold is vice president for public policy at the Guttmacher Institute. Her work concentrates on delivery and financing of family-planning services.

Megan K. Donovan is a senior policy manager at the Guttmacher Institute, focusing on access to abortion and adolescent sexual and reproductive health care in the U.S. and internationally.

Abortion and Contraception in the Middle Ages

By Roland Betancourt

Today, conversations around abortion in modern Christianity tend to take as a given the longstanding moral, religious and legal prohibition of the practice. Stereotypes of medical knowledge in the ancient and medieval worlds sustain the misguided notion that abortive and contraceptive pharmaceuticals and surgeries could not have existed in the premodern past.

This could not be further from the truth.

While official legal and religious opinions condemned the practice, often citing the health of women, a wealth of medical treatises produced by and for wealthy Christian women across the Middle Ages betray a radically different history—one in which women had a host of pharmaceutical contraceptives, various practices for inducing miscarriages, and surgical procedures for the termination of pregnancies. When it came to saving a woman's life, Christian physicians unhesitatingly recommended these procedures.

Since antiquity, the termination of pregnancies has long been associated with women at the margins of society, such as sex workers, and highlighted not only for the termination of the fetus's life, but for the great danger it posed to women. For instance, in the Hippocratic Oath, Hippocrates refuses to assist in or recommend euthanasia and additionally refuses to give women abortifacients given the danger to which they put the life of the mother.

Religiously, the Church Council of Ancyra in 314 CE stated that women found to have committed or attempted an abortion on themselves or others were to be exiled from the Church for 10 years, revising earlier suggestions that they be exiled for life. Yet, in the mid-fourth century, the Church Father Basil the Great revises these decrees, suggesting that time should not be proscriptive but dependent on the repentance of the person. There, however, he focuses not just on the fetus, but again on the danger of these procedures for women, who "usually die from such attempts."

The laws of the early Christian world generally reflected these prohibitions, outlining exile as the punishment for whomever has undertaken an abortion or aided in one—or, death if the person dies in the process. Many of these laws were codified in the sixth-century *Digest of Justinian*, a legal compendium culled from ancient legislative opinions.

Nevertheless, these legal opinions betray the real complexity that abortions had in the ancient and medieval worlds. For example, the *Digest* cites the opinion of the jurist Tryphonius, where a woman was sentenced to death for undertaking an abortion, precisely because she did so with the malicious intent of denying her husband an heir by aborting the unborn inheritor. Legally, we see abortions being intimately associated with a patriarchal control of lineage and reproduction. The *Digest* clarifies that if a woman undertakes an abortion after a divorce, "so as to avoid giving a son to her husband who is now hateful," however, she should only be temporarily exiled.

The fourth-century Church Father John Chrysostom even turned these stereotypes on their head. Though criticizing abortions, in one sermon he offers the example of a sex worker forced to have an abortion so as to not lose her livelihood. While damning the act as a murderous practice, he places blame not on the woman, but on her client, chastising the man by saying that the sex worker cannot be criticized for seeking out an abortion, writing, that while "the shameless act is hers, the cause of it is yours." Thus, it is the sex worker's client who is the cause of the murder, not she who requires her attractive body to survive.

Despite the prohibition in the Hippocratic Oath, gynecological texts were replete with recipes for contraceptive and abortive suppositories. The second-century gynecology of Soranus of Ephesus details these recipes and advocates their use for women who have a medical reason to prevent pregnancy, strongly opposing their use simply "because of adultery or out of a consideration for youthful beauty," given the health risks involved. Thus, adultery and a conceited desire to preserve one's good looks were often lodged against women known to practice abortions.

The recipes of Soranus were transmitted across the centuries in various texts, each demonstrating an active history of use and commentary. For example, in Aëtius of Amida's sixth-century medical treatise, the author details the use of contraceptive vaginal suppositories, elaborating on the improvements to the recipe from Soranus's time. There, Aëtius writes that once the contraceptive has been used, "if she wishes, [the woman] may have intercourse with a man. It is infallible because of its many trials."

Aëtius's gynecological treatise has often been associated with the patronage of the elite imperial circle of Empress Theodora in Constantinople, an empress whom the court historian Procopius once described as often conceiving, "but by using almost all known techniques she could induce immediate miscarriage." The use and efficacy of contraceptives and abortifacients extend throughout the Christian Middle Ages. In one 12th-century text from Salerno, the author offers the example of sex workers, who frequently have intercourse yet only rarely conceive.

Therefore, the medical historical evidence proposes a very different story from that told by official religious or legal texts. The fact of the matter is that good Christian women were indeed undertaking abortions and using contraceptives. Yet, wealthy and elite Christian women had not only recourse to the best medical knowledge of their era but also the privacy to undertake these practices without shame.

Most surprisingly, however, these medical practices were not only relegated to herbal, pharmaceutical contraceptives, and abortifacient drugs, but also the various surgical interventions, what today we would refer to as a late-term abortion.

In the early 10th-century *Life of Patriarch Ignatios*, by Nicetas David Paphlagon, a narrative of a religious figure, the author recounts the story of a woman in labor with a breeched birth. There, she is in immense pain and the author writes that "in order to prevent the woman too from perishing with her child, the doctors [attended] to operate on the baby and draw it out by cutting it limb by limb." While the procedure ultimately does not need to happen thanks to the miraculous workings of a relic, the author, without any moralization or shame, details here the contemporaneous procedures for an embryotomy, as described in medieval surgical manuals.

Further corroborating the continued use of this surgery, we can note that the sixth-century text by Aëtius of Amida (citing a certain Philumenos and Soranus), details the operation for an embryotomy similarly. The same operation is also recounted perfectly in Paul of Aegina's own seventh-century compendium on surgical practices.

These late-term abortions echo their modern counterpart, demonstrating that this was a known and established practice in the Middle Ages. This medical knowledge flourished in particular in the Greek-speaking, eastern Roman Empire, most commonly known to us today as the Byzantine Empire. Glimmers of the medical prowess of the Byzantine Empire and its long-thriving history are scattered across medieval sources.

In fact, one of the first recorded uses of a Caesarian section on a living woman comes down to us from Visigothic Spain, but the text tells us the deed was performed by a skilled "Greek" (aka Byzantine) doctor, who is called to save the life of a living mother whose child has died in the womb.

While Caesarians were used in antiquity, they were deployed then only to rescue a child from a dead mother. In the *Lives of the Fathers of Mérida*, composed in the 630s, the author chronicles the life of Paul, bishop of Mérida around 540/550. Paul is a Greek who had trained as a doctor in his youth. In order to save the life of a wealthy woman, he must put his clerical garments aside and sully his hands with an embryotomy. The text describes how "with wonderous skill he made a most skillful incision by his cunning use of a knife and extracted the already decaying body of the infant, limb by limb, piece by piece," in order to save the woman's life.

The only difference between the figure of the sex worker shamed for her abortions and the persons for whom these gynecological and surgical books were commissioned is that the latter were courtly elites. Therefore, they had better recourses to medical knowledge, treatment and privacy.

But, the fact that stories of late-term abortions even find their way into saints' lives without judgment belie a more important fact: that abortions undertaken for the preservation of a woman's life or health were rarely, if ever, under attack by medieval Christian authors. Not even the moralizing religious texts touch upon such cases. This is a fact that modern Christian pundits have not merely forgotten, but just never learned.

About the Author

Roland Betancourt is a professor of art history, Director of Visual Studies and a Chancellor's Fellow at the University of California, Irvine. He is the author of Byzantine Intersectionality: Sexuality, Gender, and Race in the Middle Ages *(Princeton University Press, 2020).*

Latin American Abortion Laws Hurt Health Care and the Economy—a Lesson for a Post-*Roe* U.S.

By Emiliano Rodríguez Mega

As the U.S. braces for the possible rollback of abortion rights later this year, seismic shifts are happening south of the border. A series of recent legal and legislative decisions has begun to loosen restrictions in Latin America, a region with some of the world's harshest antiabortion laws. And they could chart a path toward reform for governments that still advocate for the procedure to remain illegal. The health and economic consequences of keeping longtime bans in place may provide cautionary lessons for the U.S. as a Supreme Court decision to scrap *Roe v. Wade* appears to be imminent.

El Salvador has stood out for its aggressive pursuit of pregnant people who seek an abortion or have a miscarriage. Since 1998 the country has upheld a total ban on abortion, even in cases of rape, incest, and high-risk pregnancy. As a result, about 181 women were prosecuted between 2000 and 2019 for getting an abortion or suffering an obstetric emergency, according to data compiled by a human rights group.

A woman known only as Manuela was one of them. In 2008 she had a miscarriage and went to a hospital to be treated for serious blood loss and preeclampsia. Her physician suspected that Manuela had taken steps to willfully terminate her pregnancy and called the police. Manuela said she lost the fetus after falling into a river while washing clothes. But she was almost immediately detained. A few months later, she was sentenced to 30 years in prison for "aggravated homicide." She died in 2010, after receiving erratic treatment for Hodgkin's lymphoma.

On November 30 the Inter-American Court of Human Rights ruled that El Salvador violated Manuela's rights and was responsible for her death. The court ordered the government to provide compensation to Manuela's family and to create a number of protocols, including one that protects patient-doctor confidentiality. Morena Herrera, head of the Citizen Group for the Decriminalization of Abortion in El Salvador, says the decision is unprecedented in the region and could spark much needed changes. "It won't be automatic, I think, but recognizing that the total ban [of abortion] causes such injustices is an important step," she says. "It erodes the crime that some conservative sectors are so keen on."

The pressure on the government of El Salvador has continued following the decision of the human rights court. Three women imprisoned for obstetric complications, such as a miscarriage, were released by the government on December 23–that brings the number freed since 2009 to 60 women, a direct result of activism by human rights groups.

The court's ruling may contribute to a larger but by no means monolithic trend in which Latin America has started to decriminalize abortion. This regional shift comes just as the U.S. Supreme Court signals that it may be ready to end *Roe v. Wade*, the 1973 case that guarantees a constitutional right to the procedure.

Should that decision be overturned, at least 26 states are poised to immediately ban or acutely curtail access to abortions, according to an analysis by the Guttmacher Institute, a New York City and Washington, D.C.–based research group that supports abortion rights. "A post-*Roe* U.S. is one with dramatically expanded inequalities in abortion access," says Caitlin Knowles Myers, an economist at Middlebury College. "The result will be that about 40 percent of U.S. women who reside in a broad swath of the South and Midwest will experience the closures of nearby abortion providers."

To understand what reduced access to abortion in a post-*Roe* future could mean, some experts suggest looking at the past experiences of Latin America–and its current evolution toward an easing of bans. Many countries in the region have used abortion restrictions as a way to undermine the agency that women and others, such as transgender men and nonbinary people, retain over their body, says Mariana Romero, a researcher on reproductive health who leads the Center for the Study of State and Society in Buenos Aires. "What those laws seek is control," Romero says. "And [shaping] the perception of this autonomy [to abort] as a selfish, deviant act."

The legal status of abortion throughout Latin America confirms her view. Until recently, only a handful of smaller nations–Cuba, Guyana, and Uruguay–had decriminalized abortion. A Guttmacher report showed that more than 97 percent of women in the region lived in countries with some kind of restriction in 2017. And it found that about 760,000 of them were treated for complications from unsafe abortion each year–although the use of self-managed medication, such as misoprostol, has increased the safety of clandestine procedures.

Decades of prohibition have "allowed us to see the most terrible consequences of the disproportionate and arbitrary application of criminal law" in regard to abortion, says Carmen Martínez López, regional manager for Latin America and the Caribbean at the Center for Reproductive Rights, a legal advocacy organization based in New York City.

But the situation is in flux. In the past year alone, Argentina became the largest country in Latin America to legalize abortion for any pregnant person who requests the procedure within 14 weeks of gestation–the culmination of a years-long movement to expand abortion rights in the country. And last year the Mexican supreme court ruled that imposing criminal penalties for those who seek an abortion is unconstitutional. Chile, which had an outright ban on abortions until 2017, debated a bill to ease restrictions on the procedure. And Colombians now await a potential ruling to eliminate barriers to legal abortion and end the prosecution of people who have had an abortion. The debate over abortion intensified during the Zika outbreaks in the Americas during 2015 and 2016.

Romero was lead author of a six-country study, ranging from Argentina to El Salvador, that revealed just how disparate access still is–and how abortion persists as a major public health issue. After surveying nearly 8,000 women, her results show that nearly

50 percent of them experienced moderate complications related to pregnancy and more than 46 percent had mild ones. The rest had poor outcomes, including more than 3 percent who faced potentially life-threatening consequences and 0.2 percent who died. The study noted that restrictive policies, as well as the stigma surrounding abortion, may make the procedure unsafe.

Abortion-related complications can fall rapidly when policies are eased. In 2007, when Mexico City legalized abortion for the first trimester of pregnancy, women's health improved dramatically. There was an immediate drop in hospitalizations because of blood loss, a complication that is common following an unsafe abortion. "The magnitude of the effect is so big," says Damian Clarke, a health economist at the University of Chile, who co-authored the research. "There have been very few public health implementations where you just see that it cuts morbidity in half with just one law change."

The benefits of legalizing abortion are not only health-related. In a 2021 analysis Yana van der Meulen Rodgers, a health economist at Rutgers University, and her colleagues read through hundreds of studies that evaluated how abortion care and policies impact economies across the world, including Latin America. "Overall, we found extensive financial costs to individual women, as well as to national governments, when there are restrictive abortion laws," Rodgers says. Women, she discovered, faced higher medical costs because they tended to delay abortions and seek unsafe procedures. In Latin America, medical assistance following an unsafe abortion made up more than half of countries' budgets for obstetric care.

For Clarke, the extent of the evidence holds a message for the U.S. "At the moment, as precarious as it is, abortion is available," he says. "If this gets taken away, then we should expect a really big spike in [abortion-related] complications."

A nascent movement has begun in activist groups in Mexico to help U.S. women gain access to abortion pills. Several organizations are meeting in January to sketch a plan to distribute abortion-inducing medication in Texas, which enacted a new ban on the procedure in September. The goal is to create "a cross-border network of support for safe abortion for Texan women," says Verónica Cruz, director of the Guanajuato-based feminist organization Las Libres, which is leading the initiative. Should *Roe v Wade* be reversed, the idea is to expand this support network to other states, she adds.

Roe's potential demise could also have a spillover effect in countries where there is a tradition of harshly criminalizing abortion. Previous U.S. legislation had a similar effect. In 1984 the nation enacted the so-called global gag rule. In effect, the policy, which has been rescinded and reinstated multiple times, prohibits foreign organizations that receive U.S. funds from providing abortion counseling or advocating for decriminalization of the procedure or expansion abortion services.

In a 2018 book on the gag rule, Rodgers looked at data from more than 50 countries and found that when the U.S. restricted financial assistance to them based on whether or not they provided abortion services or referrals, abortion rates climbed in Latin America and the Caribbean, as well as in sub-Saharan Africa. "There was less financial assistance for reproductive health services, so clinics closed or had reduced staffing. They had fewer supplies," Rodgers says. This resulted in less access to contraception, more unplanned pregnancies, and more abortions, many of which were unsafe because of restrictive laws.

It is unclear yet whether *Roe*'s reversal would again cause such dramatic disruptions. But the decision would likely bolster the ideological stance of regional Latin American conservative movements and influence legislative changes. "One cannot be naive," Martínez López says, "even if one is optimistic."

About the Author

Emiliano Rodríguez Mega is a science journalist based in Mexico City.

Section 2: Sex Education and Privacy

Many States That Restrict or Ban Abortion Don't Teach Kids about Sex and Pregnancy

By Fionna M. D. Samuels

The Supreme Court's decision overturning *Roe v. Wade* in *Dobbs v. Jackson Women's Health Organization* shattered the U.S.'s already patchwork abortion coverage. States where it was once incredibly challenging to receive this sometimes lifesaving medical procedure banned it outright. In some states, old laws regained their constitutionality, while in others, lawsuits challenging abortion restrictions were struck down. Interestingly, many states that ban or severely restrict abortion are also failing to comprehensively educate their young people about safe sex.

"Sex education is designed to give people the skills, values and attitudes that empower them to have a healthy life," says Georges Benjamin, executive director of the American Public Health Association. "Those places that don't [offer] that are basically just throwing the dice and hoping that the kids will get it."

The nonprofit Sexuality Information and Education Council of the United States (SIECUS) collected data on sex education policies across the country and found that, like abortion coverage, such policies are fragmented. In fact, only 32 states and Washington, D.C., mandate sex education in schools. Of them, 15 states and Washington, D.C., mandate that abstinence-only education be included or emphasized without any coverage of contraceptives, and four states do not specify that the lessons should cover either category.

Among states that do not mandate sex education, 12 have policies in place directing that students be taught about abstinence or contraception if a school decides to provide sex education. Six states neither require sex education nor mandate teachers include these categories when it is taught.

This state-by-state variation hurts youth. "It's wildly to the detriment of young people," says Christine Harley, president and CEO of SIECUS. "We are failing young people across this country left and right." She says that people might not understand the breadth of comprehensive sex education, which is about more than anatomy and how people become pregnant. "It's about healthy relationships, teaching about how to navigate communication and negotiation, personal safety, consent, and decision-making," Harley explains.

The sex education SIECUS advocates for is trauma-informed and inclusive of all sexual and gender identities, Harley says. Such comprehensive education provides many positive health outcomes for young people. "You see young people delaying [sex], having fewer sexual partners, having fewer unplanned pregnancies, having less transmission of [sexually transmitted infections] and HIV," Harley says. "These are all things that we want for young people." Additionally, she says, there is evidence to suggest that comprehensive, evidence-based sex education helps prevent relationship violence and sexual abuse because it teaches young people what red flags to watch out for.

"Young people are smart," says Elizabeth Nash, principal policy associate for state issues at the Guttmacher Institute, a nonprofit research and policy organization that works to advance global sexual and reproductive rights. "With information and health care access, young people can make decisions for themselves." In an ongoing analysis, Guttmacher collects and evaluates state policies and classifies U.S. states on a scale from "most protective" to "most restrictive" of abortion. Now that states can and have banned abortions outright, Nash says, sex education is more important than ever. Comparing the overlap between the places where such education is the least comprehensive to those where abortion is most restricted reveals "it's basically a circle."

But banning abortion has not been the only response from states. Nash explains that in states where abortion restrictions are more of a gray area, more conservative legislatures push trigger laws through courts while more liberal-leaning legislatures are shifting toward being more protective. "We have a constitutional amendment to protect abortion rights pending in California, Michigan, and Vermont this November," she says. And there are other states deciding on money allocations for abortion funds. But this isn't enough in her opinion. "We need the federal government to step in across the board on reproductive health," Nash says—from protecting abortion to improving contraceptive access to mandating comprehensive sex education. Without comprehensive abortion protections and sex education policies at the federal level, reproductive health with continue to be wildly different across the country.

Most Protective State for Abortion and Sex Ed

Guttmacher considers Oregon the "most protective" state for abortion. "Oregon doesn't have a gestational age law," Nash says, so a person can have an abortion at any stage of pregnancy. The state also dedicates resources to providing abortion access: in March $15 million of Oregon's money was allocated to the Reproductive Health Equity Fund, which will help patients pay for both abortion services and travel costs. "Not very many states have adopted a state fund to pay for abortions"—at least not yet, Nash says.

Oregon is one of the 32 states that mandate sex education. Further, the sex education provided to young Oregonians must be age-appropriate, evidence-based, culturally appropriate and medically accurate. It is also one of the few states whose programs must be inclusive of LGBTQ+ people and include comprehensive discussions about how to maintain healthy relationships. Although the state mandates that abstinence must be emphasized in its sex education programs, there must also be expansive coverage of other contraceptive methods. "We would consider [Oregon] to be an 'abstinence plus' state," Harley says. "Despite the emphasis and the encouragement around abstinence, they're still doing the best to provide young people with as much information as possible about safer sex practices."

Least Protective States

In some ways, Nebraska's sex education policies are diametrically opposed to those in Oregon. "Sex education is not mandated," Harley says. "Whatever is taught in the classroom, there's no requirement that it be evidence-based, culturally appropriate, or medically accurate." This might lead to sex education programs that are based on religious, abstinence-only teachings. Young people in Nebraska may be taught that anything sexual outside of a "God-ordained, monogamous, heteronormative marital relationship" is a sinful activity, Harley says.

Nebraska is also a restrictive state when it comes to abortion. The medical procedure is legal until 22 weeks after the first missed period. If a person has not purchased an additional rider insurance policy that adds abortion benefits, however, neither privately nor publicly funded insurance can be used to cover it except in very limited, life-threatening circumstances. Parental consent is required for any minor seeking an abortion, and anyone who wants the procedure must wait 24 hours after their state-mandated counseling to receive treatment.

Nebraska's state legislature is in the process of restricting abortion even further and attempting a full ban. A filibuster narrowly prevented a trigger ban from passing there earlier this year. For now, Nebraskans can continue seeking the reproductive care that they need.

Abortion is also banned in Mississippi, the state that brought *Dobbs* in front of the Supreme Court. After the decision overturned nearly 50 years of medical precedent and a Mississippi judge refused to block the state's 2007 law banning abortion, it went into effect on July 7. The ban makes abortions in Mississippi illegal except in the case of rape—but only if it was reported to police officers—or when the pregnant person's life is at risk. After a lower court ruled against them, attorneys for Jackson Women's Health Organization, the state's only abortion clinic before the ban, filed a request to the Mississippi Supreme Court to block the state law on the same day it went into effect. When the higher court declined to expedite the appeal, the owner of the clinic sold the building. There are no longer any abortion clinics in Mississippi.

"If a state is looking toward banning abortion or has already banned abortion," Nash says, "then it's incredibly likely that their sex education policy is either abstinence-only or, at the very least, abstinence-focused." This is true for Mississippi. The state mandates that sex education be taught to students and that it include abstinence-only curricula. There is no requirement to cover alternative contraceptive methods. Furthermore, teachers, school counselors and nurses are not allowed to tell students that "abortion can be used to prevent the birth of a baby."

Benjamin asserts that it's only a matter of time before *Roe*'s protections are reinstated. He cites past policies that were widely unpopular, such as prohibition, as examples. "I know that our nation makes bad policy decisions on occasion." he says, "And when we do–and we have very, very terrible things that happen–the public rises up and demands that it be fixed." He sees a two-tiered approach in the wake of the *Dobbs* decision. First, abortion access needs to be protected. Second, social support needs to be in place, "which includes comprehensive sex education, making sure that [parents] have paid sick leave and making sure that we provide health insurance coverage," Benjamin says.

"Even when we reestablished *Roe*, and we will, as a law of the land," he adds, "that social agenda will still be intact and important."

About the Author

Fionna M. D. Samuels was a 2022 AAAS Mass Media Fellow at Scientific American. *She's pursuing a Ph.D. in chemistry at Colorado State University.*

Bioethics Faces a Virginity Test

By Jacob M. Appel

Two controversies related to women's virginity have recently generated controversy among physicians and medical ethicists. The first of these is a campaign in Great Britain to ban hymenorrhaphy (often referred to by the broader term hymenoplasty), the surgical repair of the hymen in an effort to convey the appearance of prior sexual abstinence. The second involves legislative efforts in California and New York to criminalize virginity testing. Both efforts are clearly well-intentioned, yet each raises complex ethical concerns.

Women's virginity has historically been valued in some religious and cultural traditions, and evidence of past sexual intercourse may render women in certain groups unmarriable. This remains true today in some Muslim communities. The issue drew international attention in 2008 when a French court in Lille annulled a marriage (a ruling later overturned) after the husband discovered that his wife had misled him into thinking she was a virgin. The absence of an intact hymen–a mucosal tissue the protects the vaginal opening–is falsely believed to be evidence of unchastity. In reality, a wide range of non-sexual activities in girlhood many lead to the rupture of the membrane, which is often asymptomatic and goes unnoticed. A British study found that the hymen may even remain intact after intercourse.

In an attempt to create the illusion of virginity, Muslim women in Europe and the United States may undergo hymenorrhaphy, a surgical procedure in which the hymen is reconstructed. The procedure began to draw significant public notice after the premiere of Davide Sordella's 2008 film *Women's Hearts*, which tells the story of a women who travels from Italy to Morocco for the procedure. Hymenorrhaphy is increasingly available in both the United States and Great Britain. It takes approximately 30 minutes to one hour and costs between $1,500 and $5,250.

The purpose of banning this procedure is to protect women from pursuing, often under duress, a medically unnecessary operation and enduring its concomitant risks including infection. This motive is certainly admirable. One might compare such a ban to the similar campaign to stamp out female genital cutting (FGC) or "female circumcision" and its criminalization in the West. Unlike FGC, however, many of the clients pursuing hymenorrhaphy are adults.

Yet banning hymenorrhaphy might have a significant downside. Unable to obtain the procedure, Muslim women may then face severe consequences from limited marital prospects to intrafamilial violence for failing to prove their virginity. Until the state can protect these women from such devastating consequences, which will likely require sustained educational efforts and a fundamental change in community values, women in these communities may be the best judges of whether or not to pursue the surgery. Nobody else can weigh as meaningfully the risks of the procedure against the risks of forgoing it. Rather than FCG, a better analogy might be made to the reporting by physicians of intimate partner violence (IPV), which many jurisdictions do not require and some do not even permit–recognizing that victims of IPV are the individuals who can best determine whether such reporting serves their own interests.

In the United States, activists are not challenging hymenorrhaphy, but rather targeting the virginity tests that make it seem necessary. The effort gained considerable traction in response to a statement by a musician known as T.I. on the podcast Ladies Like Us, in which he said that he takes his 18-year-old daughter on "yearly trips to the gynecologist to check her hymen." His claim produced widespread public backlash.

California Assemblywoman Lorena Gonzalez of San Diego has introduced legislation to prohibit hymen examinations by physicians; doing so would lead to potential disciplinary action by the state medical board. In New York State, Assemblywoman Michaelle Solages of Elmont has gone one step further; her bill would render such exams a felony. By targeting the tests, the goal is to render hymenorrhaphy both unnecessary and useless. If one cannot test for an intact hymen, having an intact hymen becomes irrelevant.

Among those organizations supporting an outright ban are the World Health Organization and the United Nations Human Rights office.

Any effort to prohibit a potential medical intervention, no matter how pernicious or unnecessary, should be approached with considerable care. Entangling the state in the physician-patient relationship is not without its own consequences and may impose serious limits on the meaningful autonomy of patients. One would not be surprised if an underground market arises in professional virginity assessors with no formal clinical training who will fill the void if physicians are excluded from the practice. Alternatively, many families may simply take women abroad for evaluation, potentially exposing them to additional dangers.

Finally, there is an argument to be made that the state should trend very lightly when intervening in the deeply held cultural and religious practices of minority groups, lest one alienate these groups further from mainstream American society. All too short a road runs from proscribing virginity tests to banning certain forms of garb or headwear.

Yet the state does have a meaningful interest in preventing physicians from engaging in procedures that serve no clinical purpose. If virginity tests actually did assess virginity, conducting them would still be an affront to Western values—but the issue of whether to prohibit them by law might prove more challenging. However, virginity tests assess virginity no more effectively than divining rods detect ground water or Ouija boards sense departed spirits. They are pseudoscience. The American College of Obstetricians and Gynecologists stated in 2007 that the procedure does not have any medical indication. Needless to say, preventing the practice of pseudoscience is one of the key reasons the state regulates physicians.

Banning hymenorrhaphy and virginity testing offer two distinct approaches to addressing the same fundamental challenge: how to protect vulnerable women from a cultural practice that most Westerners, and many of these women themselves, view as oppressive. The difference is that the former lets the consequences fall squarely on the potential victims. In contrast, banning virginity tests tackles the problem in a manner least likely to jeopardize their welfare. While in an ideal world, no need would exist for such legislative action, embracing a ban on virginity exams is the best way for the medical community to pass the ethical test it now confronts.

About the Author

Jacob M. Appel, MD, JD, MPH, is the director of ethics education in psychiatry at the Icahn School of Medicine at Mount Sinai. His latest book is Who Says You're Dead? Medical and Ethical Dilemmas for the Curious and Concerned.

Yes, Phones Can Reveal if Someone Gets an Abortion

By Sophie Bushwick

A leaked memo has revealed that the Supreme Court plans to overturn the landmark *Roe v. Wade* decision. If this does occur, so-called trigger laws already passed in 13 states—along with other laws on the way—would immediately prohibit abortions in a large portion of the country. And one of the ways courts could find people to prosecute is to use the data that our phones produce every day.

A smartphone can be a massive storehouse of personal information. Most people carry one at all times, automatically registering their daily activities through internet searches, browsing, location data, payment history, phone records, chat apps, contact lists, and calendars. "Your phone knows more about you than you do. There is data on your phone that could show how many times a day you go to the bathroom, things that are incredibly intimate," says Evan Greer, director of the nonprofit digital rights organization Fight for the Future. "If, because of these draconian laws, basic activities like seeking or providing reproductive health care become criminalized in a manner that would allow law enforcement to get an actual warrant for your device, it could reveal incredibly sensitive information—not just about that person but about everyone that they communicate with."

Even with *Roe* intact, this type of digital footprint has already been used to prosecute those seeking to terminate pregnancies. In 2017 a woman in Mississippi experienced an at-home pregnancy loss. A grand jury later indicted her for second-degree murder, based in part on her online search history—which recorded that she had looked up how to induce a miscarriage. (The charge against the woman was eventually dropped.)

Such information can be extracted directly from a phone. But doing so legally requires a judge to issue a warrant. And for this, law enforcement officials must show they have probable cause to believe a search is justified. This requirement can deter frivolous searches–but it can also be evaded with relative ease. In particular, privacy activists warn that law enforcement agencies can sidestep the need for a warrant by obtaining much of the same information from private companies. "A little-known treasure trove of information about Americans is held by data brokers, who sell their digital dossiers about people to whoever will pay their fee," explains Riana Pfefferkorn, a research scholar at the Stanford Internet Observatory. "Law enforcement agencies have used data brokers to do an end run around the Fourth Amendment's warrant requirement. They just buy the information they'd otherwise need a warrant to get."

They can also access these data by presenting a tech company with a subpoena, which is easier to obtain than a warrant because it only requires "reasonable suspicion" of the need for a search, Greer explains, not the higher bar of probable cause. "We also have seen law enforcement in the past issue [subpoenas for] incredibly broad requests," Greer says. "For example, requesting that a search engine hand over the IP addresses of everyone who has searched for a specific term or requesting that a cell phone company hand over what's considered 'geofence data,' [which reveal] all of the cell phones that were in a certain area at a certain time."

By obtaining these data in bulk–whether through purchase or subpoena–an agency can crack down on a large number of people at once. And geofence and other location data can easily reveal who has visited a clinic that provides abortion care. Greer's worry is not merely theoretical: Vice's online tech news outlet Motherboard recently reported two cases of location data brokers selling or freely sharing information about people who had visited abortion clinics, including where they traveled before and after these visits. Although both companies claimed they had stopped selling or sharing this information in the wake of the news coverage, other data brokers are free to continue this type of tracking.

Such information can be even more revealing when combined with health data. For that reason, some privacy advocates warn against period-tracking apps, which many use to stay on top of their menstrual cycles and track their fertility. When software is "tracking your period, and your period's regular, then your period is late, [the app] could certainly identify a pregnancy before someone might be aware of it," says Daniel Grossman, a professor of obstetrics, gynecology, and reproductive science at University of California, San Francisco. Government officials have in fact already charted periods to determine a person's pregnancy status. For example, in 2019 a Missouri state official said his office had created a spreadsheet to track the periods of patients who had visited the state's lone Planned Parenthood facility. In that case, the government did not obtain its information from an app, but the incident demonstrates the interest that authorities might have in such data.

Although policies vary depending on the app involved, experts say companies that produce menstrual-cycle programs generally have no obligation to keep these data private. "If it's not part of a health system, which I think most of these [apps] are not, I don't think there would necessarily be any [privacy] requirement," Grossman says. Despite the fact that these data are about personal health, they are not protected by the Health Insurance Portability and Accountability Act of 1996 (HIPAA), which protects health information from being shared without a patient's consent. "Everyone needs to understand that HIPAA, the federal health privacy law, is not the huge magic shield that many people seem to believe it is," Pfefferkorn warns. "HIPAA is actually fairly limited in terms of which entities it applies to—and your period-tracking app is not one of them. Plus, HIPAA has exceptions for law enforcement and judicial proceedings. So even if an entity (such as an abortion clinic) is covered by HIPAA, that law doesn't provide absolute protection against having your reproductive health care records disclosed to the police."

Ultimately, the vulnerability of users' phone data depends on the choices made by the companies that develop the software and apps they use. For instance, when contacted with a request for comment, a representative of the period-tracking app Clue responded, "Keeping Clue users' sensitive data safe is fundamental to our mission of self-empowerment, and it is fundamental to our business model, too—because that depends on earning our community's trust. In addition, as a European company, Clue is obligated under European law (the General Data Protection Regulation, GDPR) to apply special protections to our users' reproductive health data. We will not disclose it." In the U.S., however, many companies are not subject to GDPR's requirements—and plenty of them take advantage of their free rein to sell data on to third parties. Experts recommend that users read the privacy policies and terms of service of any given app before entrusting it with their data.

"What this exposes is that the entire tech industry's business model of vacuuming up essentially as much data as possible, in the hopes that it can be turned into profits, has created this vast attack surface for surveillance and crackdowns on people's basic rights," Greer says. "And when we start thinking about how activities that are perfectly legal right now could be criminalized in the very near future, it exposes how even very seemingly mundane or innocuous data collection or storage could put people in danger." Lawmakers have introduced privacy legislation such as the Fourth Amendment Is Not For Sale Act, which would prevent law enforcement from sidestepping the need for a warrant by purchasing information from data brokers. But this has not passed into law.

Instead of relying on the government to protect privacy, some advocates suggest it would be more effective to pressure companies directly. "I think that our best bet for carrying out systemic change now is to call on companies that are gathering this data to simply stop collecting it and to stop sharing it and to make plans for what is going to happen when the government demands it," says Eva Galperin, director of cybersecurity at the nonprofit Electronic Frontier Foundation, which promotes digital rights.

Individuals can also take steps to maintain their privacy now rather than waiting on action from either the government or the tech industry. As a first line of defense, Greer recommends locking accounts securely: protecting phones and computers with strong passwords, using password managers for other programs and turning on two-factor authentication. "These three steps will protect you from most non-law-enforcement attacks," Greer says. For those worried about law enforcement, organizations such as the Digital Defense Fund have published security guides on how to further hide one's information. Potential steps include using encrypted chat apps, privacy-centric browsers such as Tor or Brave, and virtual private networks to screen one's online communications and activity. Additionally, disabling location tracking or leaving a phone at home while visiting a clinic can protect information about one's whereabouts.

Such measures may seem unnecessary now, but Galperin warns that, without the protection of *Roe v. Wade*, the fear that our most personal information can be weaponized against us is justified. "I have spent more than a decade working with journalists and activists, people in vulnerable populations all over the world and especially in authoritarian regimes," she says. "And the most important lessons that I have learned from this work is that when rights are curtailed, it happens very quickly. And when that happens, you need to have all of your privacy and security plans in place already, because if you are making those changes after your rights have already been taken away, it is already too late."

About the Author

Sophie Bushwick is an associate editor covering technology at Scientific American.

Section 3: Abortion and Contraception

Birth Control Pills Are Safe and Simple: Why Do They Require a Prescription?

By Mariana Lenharo

As the U.S. Supreme Court prepares to announce a decision that could severely restrict abortion rights in the country, access to contraception has taken on renewed importance. Birth control pills and other hormonal contraceptives–including patches, injections, and vaginal rings–have been fully covered by almost all health insurance plans since the Affordable Care Act designated them as preventive health care. But an important barrier persists: the fact that one needs a prescription to obtain them.

"There are women who have a long wait to get into a physician's office," says Maura Quinlan, an associate professor of obstetrics and gynecology at Northwestern University who recently served as the legislative chair for the Illinois Section of the American College of Obstetricians and Gynecologists (ACOG). She says that new patients wait up to six months to get an appointment in her practice in Chicago. "The main barrier is just time and access to the provider to write the prescription," Quinlan says. "And we really believe that extra step is not necessary. Going to a pharmacy is much easier, more convenient and just as safe."

Experts in reproductive health argue that the requirement for a prescription has more to do with politics than with evidence-based medicine.

Requirements for Over-the-Counter Drugs

According to the U.S. Food and Drug Administration, in order for a medication to be sold over the counter, it must treat a condition that the user can self-diagnose. The drug must be safe, and the person must be able to use it effectively without the help of a health care provider.

Hormonal contraceptives meet these requirements. First, the need to prevent pregnancy is clearly self-identifiable. "It's very easy for someone to understand that they could potentially get pregnant and that they don't want to be," says physician Krishna Upadhya, an adolescent medicine expert and vice president of quality care and health equity at Planned Parenthood Federation of America. "Most people who use contraception can figure that out on their own."

The main concerns about contraceptives' safety are events related to venous thromboembolisms–blood clots that form in the veins and can lead to potentially serious or fatal complications.

There are two types of hormonal contraceptives: one that contains progestin (a synthetic form of the hormone progesterone) only and another that combines progestin and estrogen. And they have distinct risk profiles. Most progestin-only contraceptives are not associated with an increased risk of blood clots, according to a 2016 systematic review by researchers at the U.S. Centers for Disease Control and Prevention's Division of Reproductive Health and the Duke University School of Medicine.

Combined oral contraceptives, on the other hand, do slightly increase the risk of blood clots. In a given year, three to nine out of 10,000 women who use the combined pills will develop a blood clot, according to the FDA. Among nonusers who are not pregnant, the risk ranges from one to five out of 10,000 people per year. But these are still rare events, experts point out, especially when compared with the risk of pregnancy itself. Among pregnant people, five to 20 out of 10,000 per year will develop a blood clot. The risk jumps to 40 to 65 out of 10,000 per year in the first three months after a person gives birth. During pregnancy, blood clots more easily to help prepare the body for potential blood loss during childbirth. This natural change persists for at least 12 weeks after delivery, research shows, and may be aggravated by a person's reduced mobility after giving birth.

"There [are] a lot of medications available over the counter that are much higher risk than birth control pills," says Sally Rafie, a pharmacist at the University of California, San Diego, Health. Common painkillers such as aspirin and ibuprofen may have serious side effects, including gastrointestinal bleeding, and acetaminophen has been associated with acute liver failure.

Rather than comparing the risk of birth control pills with that of other over-the-counter medications, it makes more sense to compare the former with the risk of not being able to access birth control pills at all, Quinlan says. "The risk of blood clots, if [a person] doesn't get access to contraception and gets pregnant, is much higher."

Evidence also supports people's ability to use hormonal contraceptives safely and effectively without the assistance of a doctor, another requirement for over-the-counter medications.

Prior to prescribing birth control pills, health-care providers will check if a person has any contraindications that may increase their risk of side effects. They will ask, for example, if the person smokes, has heart disease, or might be pregnant or was recently pregnant. Research shows that people are capable of self-screening. A study by researchers in England that was published in 2008 in the *Journal of Family Planning and Reproductive Health Care*, for example, found that a group of women requesting oral contraception who self-completed a questionnaire could evaluate their eligibility just as well as their health–care providers (and were even more likely to report risk factors).

During a consultation, the clinician will also explain how to use the contraceptive, which is a pretty straightforward instruction. "I think it's actually a bit insulting to women to say that they need this sort of paternalistic figure to explain to them that they need to take one pill every day at the same time," says Anna Glasier, an honorary professor at the University of Edinburgh's department of obstetrics and gynecology and an expert in reproductive health and contraception.

Evidence suggests that access to over-the-counter birth control pills may actually make people more likely to adhere to taking them. A study that recruited oral contraceptive users living in El Paso, Tex., compared a group of people who obtained their pills at a U.S.

clinic with a group of individuals who bought their pills over the counter at a pharmacy in Mexico.

"We found that people who were getting pills in the clinics had a significantly higher likelihood of discontinuing the pill," says study co-author Daniel Grossman, a professor at the University of California, San Francisco's department of obstetrics, gynecology, and reproductive sciences. "From the interviews we did with people obtaining the pills in Mexico, they said it was just easier for them, even though it meant crossing an international border."

Based on this body of evidence, medical associations such as ACOG have been supporting over-the-counter access to hormonal contraceptives for several years. A switch to over-the-counter status is also supported by the American College of Clinical Pharmacy, a professional association of pharmacists.

Regulatory Hurdles

If birth control pills check all the requirements, why are they still not available over the counter? A potential reason is that most medicines that can be obtained without a prescription in countries such as the U.S. and the U.K. are for short-term conditions. "There's a leap to go from aspirin for headache to an oral contraceptive pill, which you expect women to take for a large chunk of their reproductive lives," Glasier says. "And that's a leap regulatory authorities have found difficult."

In order for prescription drugs to make that switch, pharmaceutical companies must submit additional information to the original FDA drug application and do studies to prove that individuals can not only understand the risks of using the particular product, but also understand how to use it effectively, an FDA spokesperson said in an email. The spokesperson added that the agency works with manufacturers to help facilitate a switch from prescription to nonprescription status. "However, any switch requires sufficient information to support the safe and effective use of the product without advice from a health professional," the spokesperson said.

Pharmaceutical companies have only started that process for birth control pills very recently (at least two companies are pursuing that switch at the moment). The FDA spokesperson said that the agency generally cannot disclose whether or not a company has submitted an application, but added: "However, once a company submits a complete prescription to nonprescription switch application, the FDA's goal for making a decision on that application is generally 10 months."

This can be a long and complicated process. Switching the emergency contraceptive Plan B, also known as the "morning-after pill," to over-the-counter status took several years. "I think that experience made pharmaceutical companies very wary of doing this, because they saw that even if you have good data showing that your product is appropriate for over-the-counter sale, it could still be blocked politically," Grossman says.

Contraceptives are also not very profitable medicines, so there is little incentive to push for making them available over the counter.

"Over and above everything else is the fact that contraception is tied up with sex and morality," Glasier says. This helps explain the strong lobby against both contraception and abortion.

"In the United States, we are facing a real crisis in terms of access to abortion and also access to other sexual and reproductive health care," Upadhya says "So it's very important that we do everything that we can to expand access to safe methods of contraception."

About the Author

Mariana Lenharo is a science and health journalist with a master's in journalism from Columbia University.

How Abortion Medications Differ from Plan B and Other Emergency Contraceptives

By Tanya Lewis

The recent Supreme Court decision overturning *Roe v. Wade*, the nearly 50-year-old legal precedent that guaranteed a constitutional right to an abortion, has people scrambling for access to medications that can end a pregnancy or prevent one.

But there is already confusion over the difference between drugs for medication abortion, which are prescribed to end a pregnancy, and emergency contraceptives (including Plan B), which are taken soon after sex and *prevent* pregnancy.

Medication abortion in the U.S. usually consists of a combination of two drugs, both taken orally after consultation with a medical provider. Approved by the Food and Drug Administration, this protocol includes the drugs mifepristone and misoprostol. They work together by causing something like a heavy menstrual period.

Mifepristone (Mifeprex), also known as RU-486, is taken within 10 weeks of a pregnant person's last period. It blocks receptors for the hormone progesterone, causing the embryo to detach from the uterine wall and the uterus's lining to break down, ending the pregnancy. Misoprostol (Cytotec), a synthetic form of a prostaglandin, a group of compounds with hormonelike effects, is taken within a day or two after mifepristone. It causes the uterus to contract and the cervix to soften, allowing the uterus to empty. Misoprostol can be taken on its own to induce an abortion but is more effective when taken with mifepristone.

In contrast, emergency contraception—sometimes called the "morning-after pill"—can be taken up to three to five days after unprotected sex or failed birth control. This kind of drug works primarily by preventing or delaying ovulation, or the release of an egg from an ovary. If ovulation has already occurred, it has been hypothesized that the morning-after pill may prevent the egg from being fertilized or implanting in the uterus, although some studies suggest it does not affect these processes. Importantly, emergency contraception cannot terminate a pregnancy, which the medical community defines as a fertilized egg that has implanted in the uterus.

"The key difference between emergency contraception and medication abortion is that emergency contraception prevents a pregnancy from occurring, while medication abortion ends a pregnancy," says Jen Villavicencio, lead for equity transformation at the American College of Obstetricians and Gynecologists.

There are several types of morning-after pills: Plan B, perhaps the most well-known, consists of the synthetic hormone levonorgestrel and works by preventing or delaying ovulation. It is available without a prescription and can be taken within 72 hours of sex (the sooner Plan B is taken, the more effective it is). It may not be effective for people heavier than about 155 to 165 pounds, however. "Plan B is not able to induce an abortion," wrote a spokesperson for Foundation Consumer Healthcare, the company that owns Plan B, in an e-mail to *Scientific American*.

Another emergency contraceptive called Ella is effective in people who weigh up to about 195 pounds. It contains a drug called ulipristal acetate, and like Plan B, it works by preventing or delaying ovulation. Ella requires a prescription and can be taken within five days of unprotected sex, but it works better the sooner it is taken.

Despite the fact that the morning-after pills do not terminate an existing pregnancy, clinics in some states may falsely interpret abortion restrictions as banning emergency contraceptives too. Saint Luke's Health System in Kansas City, Mo., initially stopped providing Plan B at its locations in the state, which has outlawed most abortions, including those resulting from rape or incest. "To ensure we adhere to all state and federal laws–and until the law in this area becomes better defined–Saint Luke's will not provide emergency contraception at our Missouri-based locations," said Saint Luke's Health System spokesperson Laurel Gifford in a statement on June 28, which was reported by the *Kansas City Star* and other outlets. But the following day the health system said it would resume providing emergency contraception.

Emergency contraception "should never be subject to laws banning abortion," Villavicencio says. "Any impact of abortion bans on emergency contraception is a misapplication of the law and a misunderstanding of the medical science."

Contraception–including emergency contraception–remains legal in Missouri and throughout the country. But situations like the one in Kansas City suggest laws restricting abortion could have a chilling effect on access to contraceptives such as Plan B. And it is not a stretch to think the Supreme Court could ultimately roll back protections for contraception in general: in his concurring opinion in the court's recent decision in *Dobbs v. Jackson Women's Health Organization*, which overturned *Roe v. Wade*, Justice Clarence Thomas wrote that the court should also reconsider other cases, including *Griswold v. Connecticut*–a 1965 decision that affirmed married couples' freedom to buy and use contraception.

For now, it is important for patients and policy makers to know the difference between medication abortion drugs, which are now illegal to prescribe in some states, and emergency contraceptives, which are legal throughout the country.

"Denying people emergency contraception will only leave more people to face the realities of unintended pregnancy without having legal abortion care as a solution," Villavicencio says.

About the Author

Tanya Lewis is a senior editor at Scientific American *who covers health and medicine.*

These Drugs Could Restore a Period before Pregnancy Is Confirmed

By Mariana Lenharo

Imagine this situation: A woman misses her period and worries she might be pregnant. She doesn't want to be, so she schedules an appointment with a health-care provider and tells them she wishes to get her period back. The provider prescribes her a course of "period pills." She gets her period again, and that's the end of it.

Such a scenario is not purely hypothetical. Period pills are the same ones used in medication abortion–misoprostol alone or in combination with mifepristone–which could imply that menstrual regulation is just another name for early abortion. But the drugs might not be considered abortion medication because the patient never learns whether they were pregnant in the first place.

A recent episode of the NPR podcast *Invisibilia* explored the ambiguity at the root of such "menstrual regulation." The discussion has gained momentum in the U.S. in the past five years mostly because of the increased threats to abortion rights, says Cari Sietstra, director of the Period Pills Project, which supports providers and organizations offering this intervention. And it could be one strategy for restoring reproductive autonomy in the wake of the Supreme Court's decision to overturn *Roe v. Wade*.

Decline and Revival of Menstrual Regulation

The practice of menstrual regulation is not new. A 1972 article in *Time* noted that the procedure, then referred to as "menstrual extraction," was "becoming medically respectable." The article said that "more and more physicians are studying it as a possibly practical method of avoiding the legal and physical hardships of abortions done later in pregnancy." At the time, modern abortion medications were not available, and the technique was performed by aspirating the contents of the uterus through a tube. With the 1973 Supreme Court decision affirming the right to abortion and the popularization of home pregnancy tests, the practice gradually fell out of use.

Sietstra says that, recently, reproductive health researchers working in countries where menstrual regulation is still a common practice, such as Bangladesh, started wondering if that option would resonate in the U.S.

Research confirmed that people in this country were open to the idea. A survey of those seeking a pregnancy test at nine U.S. health centers found that, among those who said they would be unhappy if pregnant, 70 percent would be interested in receiving period pills. The results were published in 2020 in the journal *Contraception*. In addition to potentially alleviating the stigma around abortion, period pills allow people to act quickly, even if their period is late by only a couple of days.

It is not clear how widespread menstrual regulation is in the U.S. at the moment. The Period Pills Project website has a nonexhaustive list of providers that openly offer this type of care. "Our assumption is that this is still a relatively new concept for physicians and medical providers," Sietstra says.

Physician Michele Gomez, a provider of period pills in California, says she first learned about menstrual regulation from Sietstra about a year or two ago, and "it blew [her] mind" to think that there was room for ambiguity in pregnancy. "I knew how mifepristone and misoprostol worked, from my many years of using them for medication abortions, and I knew how safe they were, so there was no reason not to start using them as period pills right away," she says. It's common for doctors to prescribe medications "off-label," using them in a way the U.S. Food and Drug Administration did not originally approve them for.

Are Period Pills Safe and Effective?

Two ongoing clinical trials are evaluating the use of period pills in the U.S. One led by Gynuity Health Projects is testing misoprostol in combination with mifepristone. And one led by the University of California, San Francisco, is testing misoprostol alone. The primary goal of both trials is to check if people with a missed period are interested in menstrual regulation and if they are satisfied with the experience afterward. "We know that for some physicians, that will be an important piece of whether or not they're comfortable prescribing it," Sietstra says. The studies are still recruiting patients, so it's not clear when results will come out.

Safety and efficacy are only listed as secondary goals in the trials, mainly because the medical literature has sufficient evidence supporting the use of those pills for medication abortion, says Jennifer Ko, one of the managers of the U.C.S.F. study and a project director at the Advancing New Standards in Reproductive Health (ANSIRH) research program. The FDA has approved the use of misoprostol in combination with mifepristone to end pregnancies up to 70 days after a patient's last menstrual period. Misoprostol alone is not approved by the FDA for this indication, but guidelines by the World Health Organization state that misoprostol can also be used alone to end a pregnancy.

The difference when the pills are used for menstrual regulation is that the patient might not be pregnant. Studies show that misoprostol has been widely used in nonpregnant people (its main indication is gastric ulcers). "If someone were to take [misoprostol], and they weren't pregnant, their symptoms would be very mild," Ko says. "There might be some discomfort in terms of cramping, or they might not feel anything at all." As for mifepristone, tolerance studies have shown that it is safe when taken by healthy nonpregnant individuals even at doses much higher than those prescribed for abortion.

Sietstra says that one question she often gets from physicians is "If they can tell someone whether or not they're pregnant, shouldn't they just go ahead and do it?"

"I think many people in the U.S., especially some medical professionals, are reluctant to accept this notion of pregnancy ambiguity. Especially given the widespread availability of at-home pregnancy tests, they see one's pregnancy status as clearly binary: one is either pregnant or not," says Suzanne Bell, an assistant professor at the Johns Hopkins Bloomberg School of Public Health. She's an author of an article published in April 2021 in *Population and Development Review*, where she and her co-author introduced the concept of productive ambiguity in fertility research.

Bell argues that the uncertainty that arises from the lack of pregnancy confirmation can be empowering in situations where pregnancy is not the desired outcome. This ambiguity opens different possibilities for how an individual could deal with a late period, including menstrual regulation.

A Legal Limbo

Samantha Gogol Lint was a law student at Harvard Law School in 2019 when she became interested in menstrual regulation and how it might fit into the legal system. "As the topic was still relatively fringe but starting to pick up speed, it seemed great to get into the research [then]," Lint says.

She concludes that from a legal perspective, menstrual regulation cannot be labeled as abortion. "Looking at how the courts have described abortion, I noticed that a piece that seemed to always be there was 'knowledge of a confirmed pregnancy' or 'intent to end a confirmed pregnancy,'" Lint says. By definition, menstrual regulation doesn't rely on a confirmed pregnancy.

Menstrual regulation also doesn't perfectly fit the concept of contraception. "It is definitely further down the line of the spectrum of available means to control reproduction," Lint says. She believes that a third category–something in between contraception and abortion–would be most appropriate for the practice.

In states where abortion is legal, menstrual regulation is clearly also legal, according to Lint. And even in states where abortion is illegal, there's no rule against a medication to treat a late period when the patient's pregnancy status is unknown. "There is no law banning or restricting menstrual regulation as such," Lint says.

Considering that providers in some of those states are reporting problems accessing those medications even for nonabortion reasons, however, it's not clear how comfortable they would be with offering menstrual regulation. "It's quite possible that this would initially fall into a gray area that might not legally count as an abortion, but state legislators would be very likely to amend laws to also make period pills illegal," Sietstra says.

At the same time, she hopes that menstrual regulation can shift the polarized abortion discussion. Embracing menstrual regulation could be a way for conservative states to give health-care providers some room to act. "Even very conservative states will need to find some way to cope with the fallout of making abortion illegal in such strict ways that they put things like miscarriage management and ectopic pregnancies into a category where physicians are afraid to act," Sietstra says. "This is bound to lead to very poor public health outcomes."

About the Author

Mariana Lenharo is a science and health journalist with a master's in journalism from Columbia University.

Pregnancy Is Far More Dangerous Than Abortion

By Adebayo Adesomo

In my medical practice, where I treat people with high-risk pregnancies, I recently treated a young woman with pulmonary hypertension. Unfortunately, this diagnosis was made late into her second trimester, well after most states allow pregnancy termination. We had to have the difficult conversation that, despite all modern medical advances, as many as one in three women with this condition will die during pregnancy. Based on that information, who should decide what level of pregnancy risk is acceptable for her? Should she? Should her government? Her case illustrates some of what's at stake, should the Supreme Court overturn *Roe v. Wade*.

The risk any person accepts in continuing a pregnancy to term exceeds that of an early safe abortion by literally an order of magnitude. If women like my patient have no other option than to carry a pregnancy to term, the United States, which already ranks last out of all developed nations in maternal health, will only deepen its ongoing maternal mortality crisis.

Forcing people to undertake these risks against their will is a fundamental violation of bodily autonomy and human rights, yet multiple states stand poised to ban almost all abortions as soon as the court revokes this right to terminate a pregancy. As noted in a recent editorial in the *Lancet*, a leading medical journal, the Supreme Court justices and their supporters who seek to abolish abortion will have "blood on their hands."

Current maternal mortality statistics from the CDC paint a sobering picture. In 2019, 754 mothers died during pregnancy. In 2020, another 850 patients died because of pregnancy-related events. For each of those women who died, 70 more suffered a serious maternal morbidity event, defined as a pregnancy-related event requiring a life-saving intervention or procedure (such as blood transfusion, surgery, or admission to the intensive care unit).

And maternal mortality is inextricably bound with race, class, and age. Women 45 years or older experienced nearly 10 times the odds of dying from pregnancy as compared to those younger than 35. Black women are three times more likely to die of pregnancy-related causes than white women. As illustrated by my patient with pulmonary hypertension, underlying medical conditions also play a role in pregnancy-related risk—and their prevalence is positively associated with lower socioeconomic status. The systemic inequities that contribute to these outcomes will further exacerbate these disparities in a post-*Roe* America. In a research letter published last year, sociologist Amanda Stevenson estimated that Black women could experience a 33 percent increase in maternal deaths after a total ban on abortions, the most of any demographic group.

Although pregnancy is not a disease, even one that is otherwise uncomplicated can go unexpectedly awry. The changes that the body undergoes during pregnancy that are needed to support an ongoing gestation are still physiologically akin to running a marathon. All of an expecting mother's organs and bodily systems are put to a nine-month endurance test. The work of the heart and lungs increases by 30 to 50 percent (or even more in a twin pregnancy!), the kidneys filter more blood, the immune system adjusts, metabolic demands increase substantially, and there are myriad other changes. The way any given individual's body reacts to these changes is unpredictable.

The controversy surrounding pregnancy termination is exceptional in its treatment of abortion as anything but a medical procedure. By juxtaposing the risks of pregnancy against the safety of abortion, the scientific backwardness of limiting access to abortion care is exposed. Allowing states to ban abortions creates many more questions than it answers: Will women with health conditions be able to exercise their reproductive health rights to protect themselves from harm? How will the treatment of other obstetric conditions such as incomplete abortions or ectopic pregnancies be affected? Lives will hang in the balance as states navigate these issues.

Even a seemingly "safe" pregnancy is not without significant risk. The decision of whether to face pregnancy's risks of complications and death should be left to the pregnant person alone. Not to their congressperson. Not to their governor. Not even to their family or physician, who can nevertheless provide support and information. The surest path to having healthy babies is ensuring healthy and willing mothers. We must fight to keep the rights to pregnancy-related decisions solely among those who bear the consequences.

This is an opinion and analysis article, and the views expressed by the author or authors are not necessarily those of Scientific American.

About the Author

Adebayo Adesomo is a fellow in the Department of Maternal-Fetal Medicine and instructor in the Department of Obstetrics and Gynecology at the University of Utah. His M.D. is from the University of Texas Health Science Center.

Section 4: Reproductive Science

What Is the Point of a Period?

By Virginia Sole-Smith

In 2007 Susan Brown encountered the repelling power of period blood. While studying what menstrual fluid might reveal about a woman's health, she wanted data from a cross section of subjects beyond the student volunteers at the University of Hawaii at Hilo, where she worked as an evolutionary psychologist. Brown's team members set up a booth near the entrance of a Walmart in downtown Hilo and hung a sign that said, "Menstrual Cycle Research." Then they waited. All afternoon women and men would spot the sign, then gingerly skirt past without making eye contact.

About six months later Brown and her Hilo colleague Lynn Morrison presented their findings at the annual meeting of the American Association of Physical Anthropologists. A wave of "nervous twittering" broke out when Morrison described carrying menstrual blood samples down the hallway of their laboratory to analyze hormone levels and other biomarkers. "The audience was fine discussing a woman's cycle in the abstract," Brown explains, "but not menstrual blood itself."

That aversion has influenced women's relationships to their own bodies as well as how the medical establishment manages women when things go wrong with their reproductive health. "Our menstrual taboo is at the core of how this science is getting done," Brown says of research on menstruation.

Or not getting done, as the case may be. It is hard to measure how much money is spent on period research, but experts agree the subject is underfunded. "It's a chicken-and-egg situation, where there's not much funding for research, so there's also not much quantifying of that lack of research," says Elizabeth Yuko, a bioethicist at Fordham University.

Yet period disorders are incredibly common. When Saudi Arabian researchers surveyed 738 female college students in a 2018 study, they found that 91 percent reported at least one menstrual problem:

some got their periods irregularly or not at all; others reported excessive levels of bleeding and pain. Different studies show that as many as one in five women experiences menstrual cramps severe enough to limit her daily life. About one in 16 worldwide suffers from endometriosis, a disease where menstrual blood and tissue migrate outside a woman's uterus and form painful lesions in her pelvic cavity. And one in 10 women has polycystic ovarian syndrome, a hormonal imbalance that disrupts a woman's cycle and is a leading cause of infertility. "You can argue we need to put our resources toward researching the life-and-death stuff," Yuko says. "But that argument falls apart because we've had no problem funding erectile dysfunction research."

Menstruation, of course, is essential to human reproduction and therefore survival. It is also one of the biological processes that makes us special because humans, chimpanzees, bats, and elephant shrews are among the only animals on earth that go through it. The vast majority of mammals signal fertility through estrus, the period when females are ovulating and display their sexual receptivity via genital swelling, behavioral changes, or pronounced alterations in body odor. The female human body, however, conceals this critical window. Instead our most visible sign of potential fertility is menstrual blood, which, ironically, appears after the fertile period has closed. The endometrial lining of the uterus thickens over the course of a woman's cycle as her estrogen level rises. If none of the eggs she releases at ovulation joins with a sperm and implants in that lining as a fertilized zygote, then levels of estrogen and another hormone called progesterone drop, triggering the uterus to shed the thickened endometrium so it can start fresh in the next cycle.

But beyond this basic picture, scientists are still struggling to understand fairly fundamental questions: Why do we share this process with at least six species of bats, for example, but not monkeys? And just what is menstrual blood, exactly? "It's quite different from regular blood," Brown notes. "We know it can't clot and is full of immune agents, but we don't know much about what they do." It is also unclear why we shed this biological tissue so dramatically when most mammals that experience estrus appear to reabsorb their endometrial linings at the end of each cycle. Even less is known about why so many women–up to 80 percent, by some estimates–experience cramps, bloating, fatigue, anger or other symptoms just before the onset of menstruation. "We know so little about menstruation," says Tomi-Ann Roberts, president of the Society for Menstrual Cycle Research and a professor of psychology at Colorado College, and what scientists do know is often badly communicated with the public. "Because of this, our attitudes toward menstruation are overwhelmingly negative. This has real consequences for how we can begin to understand healthy menstruation, as well as menstruation-related disorders and the treatment options available."

Masking Menstruation

The taboo has taken many forms. In 1920 a Hungarian-born pediatrician working in Vienna named Béla Schick published a collection of anecdotal observations: When he asked a menstruating woman to handle flowers, they wilted within minutes. When he compared the bread dough made by several women, the loaf made by the one having her period rose 22 percent less. Schick concluded that menstrual blood contained a kind of poison. By the early 1950s Harvard University scientists were referring to "menotoxins" and injecting menstrual blood into animals to observe the effects. Some of those animals died, most likely because the blood samples carried bacteria and other contaminants. Not much came of these experiments in terms of useful data, but the notion that menstrual blood contains mysterious and even dangerous properties has persisted in the scientific literature and our cultural imagination.

By the late 1950s research around menstruation had shifted to center almost entirely on preventing unplanned pregnancies at a time when maternal and infant mortality was troublingly high, especially in poor communities. In 1923 Margaret Sanger, the activist, nurse and founder of the organizations that would later become Planned

Parenthood, wrote that "Birth Control means liberation for women and for men." In 1951 she met a physiologist named Gregory Pincus, who had performed what was considered at the time to be the first in vitro fertilization of rabbits. With Sanger securing funding, Pincus set up a lab to test formulations of synthetic versions of hormones that regulate the menstrual cycle and teamed up with John Rock, a Boston obstetrician-gynecologist, to run clinical trials of the drug.

After a study of almost 60 women in and around Boston, Pincus and Rock turned to Puerto Rico to run the first large-scale trial of the drug that the U.S. Food and Drug Administration would approve in 1960 as the first oral contraceptive. They recruited 265 Puerto Rican women, many of them poor, to the study without the level of "informed consent" required today. Twenty-two percent of the participants dropped out after reporting side effects such as nausea, dizziness, headaches, and vomiting. The study's medical director argued that the pill "caused too many side reactions to be generally acceptable." Nevertheless, it went to market.

The pill was, of course, celebrated as a huge breakthrough. "It was the first form of birth control separate from sex that women could completely control," notes Elizabeth Kissling, a professor of women and gender studies at Eastern Washington University. It is impossible to overstate the freedom the pill represented for women, whose reproductive lives were otherwise largely under male control. But liberation came with a price. By the late 1960s patients across the U.S. were reporting the same symptoms documented during the Puerto Rican trial. Despite many reformulations over the ensuing decades, side effects remain a problem for many women on the pill; risks for breast cancer, blood clots, and stroke may also be higher. In their quest to bring reproductive freedom to women, Sanger, Pincus, and Rock appear to have ignored the implications of shutting down a woman's natural cycle, Kissling explains. In other words, scientists figured out how to supplant periods long before they began trying to understand why they work the way they do.

It was not until the late 1980s that scientists really began to grapple with the larger question of why menstruation happens at all.

As an undergraduate, evolutionary biologist Beverly I. Strassmann wrote a paper on how concealing ovulation could entice more paternal partners. (Because a woman's fertile window is more or less invisible, it encourages what researchers call pair-bonding: human males invest in fewer sexual relationships and protect and care for the resulting offspring as a way to ensure their paternity.) Strassmann, now a professor of anthropology at the University of Michigan, wanted to explore human attitudes toward menstruation by collecting data in a community where women spend five nights of their period sleeping in huts that are separate from the rest of the tribe.

In 1986 Strassmann moved to Mali to conduct field research on the Dogon, an ethnic group of millet farmers that hew to their traditions. Dogon people who continue to practice their indigenous religion believe that a menstruating woman's presence would desecrate the religious objects in the family compounds. Researchers had not previously considered that these religious beliefs were rooted in any kind of reproductive agenda. But, as Strassmann explains, she hypothesized that this was "a cultural pattern embedded in religion that did directly serve reproduction." Although research on modern indigenous communities can offer only clues about how humans lived thousands of years ago, Strassmann hoped to show that long-standing cultural taboos around menstruation had developed to support our larger evolutionary goals.

During her initial fieldwork, Strassmann studied the community's use of menstrual huts for almost three years, collecting urine samples from 93 women to test hormone levels and prove that their use of the huts correlated with actual menstruation patterns. She also observed how quickly most of the women got pregnant again after their visits to the huts. Although the practice was ostensibly about keeping menstruation sequestered, the huts themselves were located in full view of a shade shelter used by men in the community. So the huts made a woman's fertility status clear to her husband and his family whether she liked it or not. (As noted earlier, women enter their "fertile window" after their period.)

In their quest to bring reproductive freedom to women, scientists figured out how to supplant periods long before they tried to understand why they work the way they do.

Other religious practices around menstruation, such as the Orthodox Jewish purification ritual of sending menstruating women to mikvah baths, can also be traced to men's need to track female fertility and schedule sexual activity accordingly. And although the advent of the pill means that many women can now control their reproductive life in ways that render the purpose of such practices moot, the taboos still persist, Roberts says. "We still think of menstruation as something that women have to keep hidden and separate."

Period Evolution

Although Strassmann's work was primarily about understanding the biological underpinnings of menstrual taboos, her data also revealed important characteristics about the process of menstruation itself. Perhaps her most oft-cited finding was published in 1997 in *Current Anthropology*: across human history, menstruation has been a rather infrequent event. That is because women tend to get pregnant earlier, have more babies, and spend more time breastfeeding in communities where birth control is unavailable or difficult to access than they do in communities with high rates of birth-control usage. "We think of periods as happening 12 times a year, but if you're pregnant and then nursing for extended time frames, that's a stretch of two or three years for each child when you're not menstruating," Strassmann explains. Her data showed that in the 1980s the average Dogon woman menstruated only around 100 times in her life, compared with the average American woman's experience of as many as 400 periods in her lifetime. And Dogon women's experience is closer to what all women would have experienced throughout history before the development of the pill.

This historical infrequency of menstruation helps to explain why humans evolved to do something as potentially disadvantageous as releasing blood–losing iron, protein, and other nutrients and probably attracting predators in the process. It could also help explain why periods and the week before their onset can be so unpleasant for many women. Michael Gillings, a professor of molecular evolution at Macquarie University in Australia, became interested in women's experiences of premenstrual symptoms (PMS) when premenstrual dysphoric disorder (PMDD) was added to the fifth edition of the *Diagnostic and Statistical Manual of Mental Disorders* in 2013.

PMDD is defined as severe irritability, depression, or anxiety in the week or two prior to menstruation, with symptoms easing two or three days after menstruation begins. But Gillings, along with many feminist scholars, balked at the characterization of mood swings as disordered. "Up to 80 percent of women report these symptoms; that makes PMS normal, not a psychological disorder," he says. "So we have to ask, 'Was there, at some point in history, an advantage to having these symptoms?' " In 2014 he published a paper in the journal *Evolutionary Applications* arguing that PMS offered a selective advantage because it caused tension between pair-bonds and therefore might help women dissolve relationships with infertile men. "It is difficult to prove a hypothesis like this," he acknowledges. And the media response characterized him as insensitive to the suffering of women. "I was burned in effigy on five continents," he says. Some researchers counter Gillings's claim that PMS is a product of evolution–and contend that its roots are more cultural than biological because it manifests differently around the world. Roberts sees the concept mostly as one influenced by the menstrual taboo and a way to dismiss women's emotions.

Scientists are also divided over whether the act of bleeding itself serves an evolutionary purpose. "It's never made sense to me that we have this free-flowing blood, while other animals reabsorb it," Brown argues. Many evolutionary biologists now think that the essential feature of women's cycles is not the bleeding but rather the ability of the uterus to thicken its lining in preparation for implantation and then dispose of the endometrium when it is not needed. "A healthy endometrium requires constant metabolic support, so it is less energy-intensive for the female body to tear down and rebuild it each cycle than it is to maintain it in a constant state of readiness for embryo implantation," Strassmann explains. Human circulation happens to result in a particularly bloody endometrium. "Our physiology doesn't permit reabsorption, so much of the blood gets discharged as menstruation," she says. Bleeding may therefore be an insignificant by-product of evolution rather than an advantage.

A World without Periods?

If the act of shedding menstrual blood poses no clear health benefit or evolutionary advantage and if, historically, women have not even done it all that often, then why, in this postpill era, do women continue to do it all? The answer: some do not. In early 2019 the Royal College of Obstetricians and Gynecologists in London released new guidelines that approved skipping the placebo pills in birth control to reduce the frequency of periods or avoid them altogether.

Although this formal acknowledgment is new, the practice is not. Medical menstrual suppression has long been embraced by clinicians, the media and women frustrated by the pain, mood swings, or inconvenience of their menstrual cycle. The pharmaceutical industry also took notice: as the researcher who first measured and quantified the frequency of human menstruation, Strassmann has been asked to present her data to drug manufacturers, who have offered several versions of the pill and other forms of contraception that are formulated to let women skip their periods more often, if not avoid them altogether.

Skipping that monthly ordeal can mean avoiding debilitating pain, prolonged heavy bleeding, migraines, and other symptoms that can dramatically impair a woman's quality of life. The approximately 25 percent of reproductive-age women and girls who struggle with additional kinds of severe menstrual pain may be at increased risk for developing other chronic pain conditions. "We suspect the cyclical experience of monthly menstrual pain somehow alters how some women process all kinds of pain," explains Laura Payne, who directs pain research at McLean Hospital and Harvard Medical School.

To many doctors faced with patients whose periods cause problems, "the pill is the closest thing we have to a panacea in women's health," says Jonathan Schaffir, a director at the Ohio State University Wexner Medical Center. But is it? "The pill isn't a treatment for these conditions," Kissling says. "It's a way of refusing to treat them." It can take up to a decade or longer from disease onset for a woman to be diagnosed with endometriosis, for example, in part because doctors are so quick to prescribe the drug to teenagers reporting bad cramps without investigating to see if there is an underlying cause, says endocrinologist Jerilynn Prior of the University of British Columbia. And where one version of the pill may succeed in masking a woman's symptoms, another may exacerbate them. "You can spend years jumping from one pill to another, not finding relief," notes Kissling, who published a paper on how women end up "treating each other," for better or worse, in online forums, where they share alternative medicine remedies and other tips out of frustration with their doctors' limited repertoire.

Strassmann and many others are skeptical about the health effects of medically induced menstrual suppression, which may expose women to hormone levels higher than what they would have experienced in the evolutionary past or even now, when regularly cycling on the pill. "It's true a monthly menstrual period is not necessary," she says. "But taking more progestin to skip your period is not living like our ancestors did 500 or 1,000 years ago." Research shows taking the pill reduces the risk for endometrial and ovarian cancers but slightly raises the risk for breast cancer, stroke, and blood clots.

In 2017 Strassmann and her colleagues published a paper in *Evolution, Medicine, & Public Health* tracking how exposure to synthetic hormones varied depending on the type of birth-control pills used. "We know that American women experience more periods than the Dogon because they start menstruating earlier and have fewer children, and we know that having more periods is associated with a higher breast cancer risk," she explains, noting that the relation is likely because of the additional hormone exposures accrued from those extra periods. "But we don't really know how that risk squares with the hormone exposure women are also getting from long-term use of birth-control pills." After analyzing data from 12 studies, as well as the information on birth-control package inserts, Strassmann's team concluded that some types of the pill exposed women to a quadruple dose of progestin (a synthetic form of progesterone contained in the pill), relative to the progesterone their naturally cycling body would produce.

Nobody knows for sure what that exposure to synthetic hormones will mean long term for women using the pill to suppress their cycles indefinitely. This knowledge gap speaks to broader concerns about our ignorance around menstruation. If Rock and Pincus had begun their work with a deeper understanding of menstruation's evolution and purpose, how might that have affected the pill's development? Would women today have more–and more targeted–options to manage their menstrual pain and associated disorders?

In this latest iteration of our menstrual taboo, dispatching with the period instead of researching its complexity might have unforeseen health consequences, Prior says. "Our data on the pill come from generations of women who followed the schedule for 28-day cycles and didn't stay on it for nearly as long as women do today," Kissling says. "What we have now" with women using birth control for long-term suppression "is the largest uncontrolled medical experiment on women in history."

About the Author

Virginia Sole-Smith is the author of The Eating Instinct: Food Culture, Body Image and Guilt in America. *Her next book,* Fat Kid Phobia, *will explore weight stigma and childrens' health.*

Why Are Girls Getting Their Periods So Young?

By Virginia Sole-Smith

Three weeks before her eighth birthday, Josie got her period at school. Magen, her mother, stopped at a drugstore for supplies before picking up her daughter. In the tampon aisle, she found a shelf of "tween" menstrual pads promising to "fit smaller bodies." She remembers thinking, "How does this even exist as a product?"

Magen was heartbroken that her seven-year-old was menstruating but not completely surprised. She had begun to notice her daughter's body odor when Josie was six. By the time Josie turned seven, she was getting blackheads on her nose, slamming doors, and sleeping late. She developed breast buds the summer before second grade. "That was traumatizing for both of us," Magen says.

Magen showed Josie how to put a pad in her underwear and then called the pediatrician, expecting to be referred for some kind of hormonal testing. Instead, Magen recalls, "he said, 'Yes, this happens. She likely won't be regular for a while, but she's very clearly in puberty at eight years old.'"

The average age of menarche, or a girl's first period, in the U.S. is now 12, according to the most recent data from the Centers for Disease Control and Prevention's National Health and Nutrition Examination Survey, down from 14 a century ago and as much as six months earlier than 20 or 30 years ago. But puberty does not start with menstruation. The onset of breast development, or thelarche, tends to come first, just as Josie experienced. "We're now seeing thelarche occur 18 months to two years earlier than we did a few decades ago," says Frank Biro, who studies problems related to pubertal maturation at Cincinnati Children's Hospital Medical Center. His research, published in 2013 in the journal Pediatrics, put the average age of breast development at 8.8 years old for African American girls, 9.3 for Hispanic girls, 9.7 for Caucasians and 9.7 for Asian Americans. "The age of breast development has clearly dropped, while the age of menarche has drifted down. They are both concerning," he says.

One popular misconception about menarche is that it represents the onset of ovulation; in fact, most girls do not begin ovulating regularly for up to two years after their first period, which is why early ones can be light and irregular. Menarche is instead triggered by changes in a girl's estrogen levels. The most probable explanation for why periods and breast development might be happening younger is that girls tend to weigh more today than they did a generation ago—and this higher body fat percentage is leading to earlier activation of the pituitary gland, which produces the hormones responsible for puberty.

In Biro's study, a higher body mass index (BMI) was the strongest predictor of early breast development across all racial groups, although the relation was correlative, not causal. "What we need to ask is, why has BMI gone up?" he says. "Decreased physical activity and a more calorically dense diet are probably part of the puzzle. But I think another critical piece is our ubiquitous environmental exposure to endocrine-disrupting chemicals," or EDCs. This class of chemicals (including phthalates, bisphenol A, and others) is used in many consumer products (shower curtains, plastic bottles, couch cushions) and has been shown to mimic estrogen and other naturally occurring hormones in the human body. Biro theorizes that some of these chemicals may promote weight gain or contribute to early puberty by influencing how cells and the body regulate metabolism, which then affects estrogen production. He is currently leading a study tracking the growth and development of 379 girls from age six onward that has been examining relations between their pubertal development and environmental exposures. Trauma could be another explanation: "Stress can also change your estrogen levels," Biro says.

Josie's mom found a shelf of "tween" menstrual pads promising to "fit smaller bodies." She remembers thinking, "How does this even exist as a product?"

To Magen, the more pressing question is not why Josie started puberty so early but rather what this means for her daughter's immediate and long-term health. The data Biro is collecting now show that girls who start puberty early tend to stay in the stage longer, meaning they spend more time in a "window of susceptibility"—a time when the human body is in a particularly critical stage of development, such that environmental exposures and other experiences are more likely to have an impact on their later health. When it comes to future risk of breast cancer, for example, fetal development and infancy are one window, and puberty is the other. "We know that for every year you delay menarche, you decrease the risk of premenopausal and postmenopausal breast cancer by 4 to 8 percent," Biro says. "On a population basis, that's really important."

Other researchers are looking at how early puberty affects girls socially and emotionally. "We know that early reproductive development is not matched by early cognitive development," says Marcia Herman-Giddens, an adjunct professor of maternal and child health at the University of North Carolina's Gillings School of Global Public Health. "So how do we teach children to manage sexual urges and other realities of puberty? And of course, these girls have to deal with sexual advances from older boys and even men long before they are ready to navigate that."

Magen is trying to figure out how to introduce these issues to Josie in an age-appropriate way without overburdening her already anxious daughter. "I've had to tell her, 'At some point, you're going to feel interested in relationships and sex, and when you are, you need to tell me right away,'" she says. "But am I really going to have to put a 12-year-old on birth control to make sure she's safe?"

About the Author

Virginia Sole-Smith is the author of The Eating Instinct: Food Culture, Body Image and Guilt in America. *Her next book,* Fat Kid Phobia, *will explore weight stigma and childrens' health.*

Pausing Fertility: What Will Happen When the Eggs Thaw?

By Liza Mundy

Sprightly yellow seems to be the hue of choice for corporate wellness chains designing a logo to attract health-minded women. There is the cleansing grapefruit of SoulCycle, the happy buttercup of Drybar. And in 2019 vans started materializing at busy pedestrian spots in Manhattan and Los Angeles that sported the shade of sunflowers. These vans are mobile fertility clinics, inviting women to pop in and learn how to safeguard their reproductive germ line by freezing their eggs. "Own your future," the ads on the side promise. "Your fertility, understood."

The vehicles are emissaries of Kindbody, a boutique fertility practice that courts the same clientele that frequents spin classes and blow-dry bars. It is one of a small but growing number of outfits that offer fertility services, including retrieving a woman's eggs, or oocytes, to be frozen for later use. Because eggs are one of the most important factors in female fertility, and both their quality and quantity declines with age, banking eggs promises to lengthen a woman's window of fertility and postpone the decision of whether to have kids. As a rival service, Extend Fertility, puts it, "Women have more options today than ever before. And we're giving you one more–the option to start your family when you're ready."

The appearance of boutique egg-freezing outfits is one of the most high-profile–but not the only–recent developments in assisted reproductive technology, which is the science (and commerce) of helping people have the babies they want. These stand-alone clinics exist thanks to a convergence of female financial empowerment, venture capital backing and real medical progress. And it is not just mobile clinics behind the push. Egg freezing is on the rise at gold-standard fertility clinics, such as the one at the University of Southern California. There, according to clinic director Richard Paulson, it accounts for almost 40 percent of egg-retrieval cycles–in which women inject themselves with hormones to stimulate their ovaries to release multiple eggs, and doctors then collect those eggs while the women are under anesthesia. (The other 60 percent of cycles at the clinic involve women undergoing infertility treatment who intend to use the eggs soon.)

Ultimately these providers are making the case that egg freezing has come far enough to justify the $10,000-plus bet women place by investing in the procedure and medications not covered by insurance (that price tag does not include the storage fees women must pay yearly to keep the eggs on ice). This confidence stems from significant breakthroughs in the science of fertility and conception made over the past decade, notably a process that allows doctors to flash-freeze eggs. Physicians have also come a long way in the science of in vitro fertilization (IVF)–the process that comes after egg freezing–which unites a thawed egg (or a fresh one) with a sperm for conception in a petri dish and then grows the resulting embryo to the point where it can be put back inside a woman's uterus to implant.

All this amounts to a sea change in the science of making babies, one that suggests, in theory, that women are not bound by the traditional notion of the ticking biological clock. Yet in practice, the reality is more complicated. Women must consider other factors besides their eggs, such as their overall health and the health of the sperm they plan to use, in deciding when to get pregnant. And just how good of a bet these new technologies truly are remains to be determined: the vast majority of frozen eggs at clinics have yet to be thawed. The question remains: Will they all be viable? Can science really safeguard fertility for later?

The Freezing Boom

In some places, such as the San Francisco Bay Area, the rise in egg freezing is linked in part to nearby tech companies such as Facebook and Google, which now (and with some fanfare) cover the procedure for employees. In Silicon Valley, egg freezing has become part of the benefits package a prudent career woman may consider availing herself of, a kind of 401(k) for future family formation. The boom also stems from other converging trends. One is the millennial generation's comfort with social media; boutique clinics have strong presences on Instagram and Twitter, as do a growing number of traditional clinics. Even online dating–which has sold the hope that much messiness of the human heart can be solved by downloading an app–has an impact. "Women have said to me, instead of looking at every date as 'Is this someone I could marry?' they can set that aside," says Marcelle Cedars, director of the University of California, San Francisco's Center for Reproductive Health.

The rise in freezing also bespeaks a public inured to paying a monthly fee for products. What egg freezing is–among other things–is one more paid-subscription service, like Netflix or Zipcar. Oocytes, once frozen, must be kept frozen until used. After a woman goes through the not easy or cheap process of having eggs retrieved, she will be powerfully motivated to continue paying the storage fee, which can be as much as $500 or $1,000 a year. Every batch of eggs in liquid nitrogen represents an income stream for years, for the clinic and its investors.

But the freezing trend is also the outcome of science. Asked to reflect on stages of progress in the field, Paulson casts his mind back to when in vitro was in its infancy. The first IVF baby was Louise Brown, born in 1978, now a mother herself. The technology for the scheme was nonexistent to the point where doctors had to fashion their own utensils to retrieve eggs and incubate embryos; when the late gynecologist Patrick Steptoe and the late physiologist Robert Edwards were performing the experiments that would result in Brown's birth, they kept embryos warm in a pouch created in the skin of a living rabbit.

Into the 1980s IVF patients could expect, at best, a 10 to 15 percent delivery rate. "We were able to help a handful of people," says Alan Penzias, an associate professor at Harvard Medical School and a doctor at Boston IVF. "But not the majority. Most people failed."

The retrieval of eggs–the well-protected female germ line–has always been hard. The 1980s saw basic techniques developed and refined; at first, doctors had to perform laparoscopic surgery to extract a single egg the instant it was ovulated. They learned to administer hormones that could cause eggs to ovulate in greater quantity and at a more predictable time and to retrieve them vaginally, with a needle that pokes through to the ovaries. The 1990s were–unexpectedly–the decade of the man. Male-factor infertility–slow or misshapen sperm or low sperm count–is a common reason couples may be unable to conceive. For a long time the only "cure" for male-factor infertility was sperm donation. Then, in 1992, scientists in Belgium announced the first live birth after using ICSI–intracytoplasmic sperm injection–in which a single sperm is injected into the egg. ICSI was a disruptive technology that cured male-factor infertility, for couples who can afford it.

For more than half a century it has been almost ridiculously easy to freeze sperm, which are stripped-down DNA missiles. The first reported human birth from frozen sperm occurred back in 1953. Not so for the egg, which is among the largest cells in the body and difficult to freeze well. Eggs are mostly water, meaning ice crystals can form, with sharp edges that damage organelles and other delicate structures. For years freezing an egg entailed dehydrating it to the fullest extent possible, then introducing tiny amounts of cryoprotectant, a kind of antifreeze that aims to prevent crystals from forming. Everything was done very slowly. "It would be this painful process that would take about two to three hours," says Amy Sparks, an embryologist at the University of Iowa, who remembers the agony of ratcheting down the temperature bit by bit. This technology enabled the first human birth from a frozen embryo in 1984; the first birth from a frozen oocyte was reported two years later, in 1986. But for eggs, freezing remained both difficult and damaging: the upshot often was like what happens when you thaw ice cream and refreeze it: icy granulation. "When it thaws, all of a sudden the water from those crystals has nowhere to go and causes damage to the cell," Sparks says.

Then, about 10 years ago, came the most important recent scientific breakthrough in assisted reproductive technology. Vitrification—from *vitrum*, Latin for "glass"—is the ability to freeze eggs (and embryos) breathtakingly fast. The procedure involves larger quantities of cryoprotectant than earlier methods and a direct plunge into liquid nitrogen, which triggers "ultrarapid cooling," minimizes the formation of ice crystals and almost instantly transforms the egg into a glasslike state. "In the past 10 years the impact of vitrification ... has really transformed the field in ways that we could not have foreseen," says Serena Chen, director of the clinic at Saint Barnabas Medical Center in New Jersey.

Vitrification is akin to pushing the "pause" button, Chen says; when the time comes, the laboratory pushes "play" and commences rapid thawing. The results are so show-stopping that in 2018, the ethics committee of the American Society for Reproductive Medicine (ASRM)—which up to that point had declined to recommend social use of the technology—issued a paper saying egg freezing "for women attempting to safeguard their reproductive potential for the future" could now be considered "ethically permissible." In short: egg freezing has gone mainstream. Clinics disagree over whether frozen eggs are as viable as fresh, but most experts, including Paulson and Sparks, say they are very, very close. And there is no question that eggs frozen when a woman is 32 are better than fresh eggs retrieved from the same woman at 42.

But even great eggs, just like sex, do not always make a baby. Cedars explains to patients that they should not wait to use frozen eggs until their early 40s, because if they do not work, the old-fashioned method might not either. Yet here lies a quandary—if women cannot wait until their fresh eggs have declined, what is the point of freezing in the first place?

IVF Strides

Vitrification is not the only advance helping to buoy the promise of egg freezing. Other elements of IVF have seen major improvements, such as the new standard of growing an embryo for five days in the lab before transferring it back to a woman. A decade ago embryos were often transferred at the three-day stage, when they consisted of just eight cells. Human embryos now arrive in the uterus as "blastocysts," with roughly 100 cells, which are more mature and robust and have a much greater chance of success. According to CDC data from 2016, for women younger than 35, nearly 50 percent of fresh embryos transferred at day five resulted in a live birth as compared with 34.4 percent of embryos transferred at day three. For women between 35 and 37, the percentages were 42.1 for day five versus 28.6 for day three.

Success rates are also getting better because labs can now closely replicate the chemical environment of the fallopian tube, where embryos spend their first five or so days when pregnancy happens naturally. Labs have gotten much better at regulating the amounts and concentrations of nitrogen, oxygen, and carbon dioxide. Current incubators also feature more solid-state technology that requires less opening and closing of doors so that embryos can rest undisturbed.

The ability to develop embryos to the blastocyst stage means embryologists can more easily recognize the best of the batch before deciding which to try to implant. These judgment calls are also improved by a process called preimplantation genetic selection. Back in the three-day-embryo era, if scientists wanted to gauge the genetic health of an embryo, they had to pry one cell from an eight-cell mass, a lab procedure so harrowing that Sparks still has "nightmares" about it. Now it is much easier to use lasers to grab a couple of cells from the part of the blastocyst that will create the placenta–the less vital section than the one that is destined for the fetus.

All in all, embryologists' improved ability to freeze and test embryos amounts to "a huge change," Penzias says. About 10 years ago, frozen embryos had a 10 percent lower success rate than fresh. "Now we're talking about parity," he says. The improved odds mean, in theory, that whether women are using embryos created from eggs retrieved the same month or from those frozen years before, clinics can transfer just one embryo at a time rather than the two or three that used to be the norm. For 14 years it has been the University of Iowa's policy that if a woman is younger than 38, has no prior failed transfers at the clinic, and has at least a single good-looking blastocyst (a five-day-old embryo), then one is "all they get," Sparks says. These trends have reduced the prevalence of twins, and especially of triplets and higher-order multiples, which are much riskier pregnancies than carrying singletons, for both babies and moms. At the University of Iowa, the rate of twin birth used to be 40 percent in 2001; now it is under 5 percent. Industrywide, according to the CDC, the portion of transfers involving a single embryo has more than tripled, from 12 percent in 2007 to 40 percent in 2016. Equally important: the percentage of fresh single-embryo transfers resulting in a live birth increased from 21 percent in 2007 to 37 percent in 2016.

These innovations are just the beginning. A new invention allows a woman to incubate embryos inside a device inserted in her vagina rather than an incubator in the lab. And even more radical technologies are on the horizon: Mitochondrial replacement therapy, for instance, is a controversial procedure that can eliminate the risk of genetic mitochondrial disease by injecting the nucleus of a mother's egg into an egg from a woman without the disease whose nucleus has been removed but whose mitochondria remain. The procedure is banned in the U.S., out of concerns about mixing the DNA of two women, but is being developed in England. The day is also coming, Paulson says, when it will be possible to use stem cell technology to manufacture sperm and eggs from normal body cells, such as skin cells. Although it sounds like science fiction, the procedure would involve no changes to a cell's DNA, so that part, at least, is less worrisome than mitochondrial transfer. With this technology, women would no longer need to bank eggs. "At 45, you can still have an egg made out of your skin cells," Paulson says. It sounds wild, but so did IVF 40 years ago. "It's going to happen."

Ticking Clocks

It is a fact that a woman is born with all the oocytes she will have; over time her ovarian reserve diminishes, as does the quality of her eggs.

Talking about this subject has always been fraught. Back in 2001, when the ASRM launched an ad campaign partly about age-related infertility, the National Organization for Women attacked it as coercive and antifeminist. Chen says this reaction does women a major disservice; older eggs are more likely to be chromosomally abnormal, with a higher risk for miscarriage and the grief that follows. She adds that egg freezing is often depicted as elective and narcissistic, "kind of like plastic surgery or getting a cute Mini Cooper." But women face many pressures, particularly in their mid-30s, when each year of delayed childbearing means an increase in earning power. "It's not about women just being selfish and trying to work on their careers," Chen says. "The truth is, a lot of people just haven't found the right partner."

Still, Chen shares concerns about the commercialization of a technology that originally aimed to help cancer patients preserve fertility during treatment. Jake Anderson-Bialis, co-founder of the consumer education Web site FertilityIQ, worries that women do not realize taking hormones and then undergoing retrieval is not a minor lunch-hour-type procedure. And there is still no guarantee the eggs will result in a live birth. The backlash could be huge if many of the women now freezing their eggs later attempt to use them, only to find out their investment failed. The dirty secret of the fertility industry, up to now, has been multiple births; going forward, Anderson-Bialis says, "if there's going to be a black eye, it's egg freezing." By this, he means the danger that the eggs, once thawed, will not be viable–a potentially devastating outcome to women sold on the promise of egg freezing. Cedars agrees that some women are too bullish on what technology can accomplish. "We have to repeatedly say to patients, 'There's not a baby in the freezer,'" she says. "'There is the *potential* for a baby.'"

Referenced

The Biology of Menstruation in Homo sapiens: Total Lifetime Menses, Fecundity, and Nonsynchrony in a Natural-Fertility Population. Beverly I. Strassmann in *Current Anthropology*, Vol. 38, No. 1, pages 123–129; February 1997.

Report from Nine Maternal Mortality Review Committees. Building U.S. Capacity to Review and Prevent Maternal Deaths, 2018. http://reviewtoaction.org/Report_from_Nine_MMRCs

Mature Oocyte Cryopreservation: A Guideline. Practice Committees of the American Society for Reproductive Medicine and the Society for Assisted Reproductive Technology in *Fertility and Sterility*, Vol. 99, No. 1, pages 37–43; January 2013.

Preventing Unintended Pregnancy: The Contraceptive CHOICE Project in Review. Natalia E. Birgisson et al. in *Journal of Women's Health*, Vol. 24. No. 5, pages 349-353; May 14, 2015.

About the Author

Liza Mundy is a journalist, a senior fellow at the New America foundation and a former staff writer for the Washington Post. *She is author of four books, most recently the* New York Times *best seller* Code Girls: The Untold Story of the American Women Code Breakers of World War II *(Hachette Books, 2017).*

The Future of Sexual Reproduction

By Karen Weintraub

The mice scurrying around their cage in Katsuhiko Hayashi's laboratory do not look remarkable. They run, eat, and sleep like others of their kind. But these eight rodents have an unusual origin story, one that Hayashi, a reproductive biologist at Kyushu University in Japan, revealed three years ago in the pages of *Nature*. The tawny-colored mice, he and his colleagues announced, did not spring from the mating of sperm and egg. On their mother's side, their roots trace to a reprogrammed skin cell.

The advance, called "amazing" by other researchers, delivers on a promise hinted at in 1997, when scientists managed to clone Dolly the sheep. That accomplishment built on earlier cloning work in frogs from the 1970s and taught scientists that every animal cell has the same basic set of instructions. By transforming a sheep's mammary cell into a living animal, Dolly's creators showed that every mammalian cell has the same genes–and that the difference between a breast cell and any other cell is simply which genes are turned on or off.

For Hayashi and other scientists, that work created the prospect that they might be able to reprogram mammalian cells to become anything from a neuron to an egg if only they could devise the right instruction manual. A small number of researchers around the world, including Hayashi, are using this legacy to tackle in vitro gametogenesis–generating eggs and sperm from adult cells.

Reproductive scientists and some couples struggling with infertility are closely tracking Hayashi's progress, as well as similar efforts that have successfully converted rodent stem cells (progenitor cells that can develop into any type of specialized cell) into rudimentary sperm. If these egg and sperm techniques can be made to work in humans, we may one day be able to replace our faulty gametes with blood or skin cells. In that future, men would not have to worry about a lack of healthy sperm. And instead of watching their chances of motherhood fade with their 30s, women of virtually any age could give a little blood and end up with a batch of eggs. Gay couples, too, might one day be able to have children to whom they are both biologically related.

The hope remains tantalizing but distant. Years of animal experiments aimed at finding a reliable substitute for the egg and sperm cells essential to creating most mammalian life have not yet succeeded. But even this very preliminary work in mice and human cells is prompting a wave of ethical questions from the scientific community about eventual human applications.

Planning Parenthood

To make this reproductive process work in mice, Hayashi's team needed to tie together several earlier discoveries. In 2010 it practiced hitting the "reset" button on cells, sending them back to a stage before they had found their identity. The team began by retracing a process developed by Shinya Yamanaka of Kyoto University in Japan, for which he won a Nobel Prize in 2012.

First, the researchers scraped skin cells off an adult mouse's tail. They then injected them with a chemical cocktail containing four specific genes to transform adult cells back into stem cells capable of becoming many different kinds of cells. Next, they employed genetic insights established in the early 2000s by Azim Surani of what is now the Gurdon Institute in England and Mitinori Saitou, who was then working in Surani's lab. (Both men would later mentor Hayashi.) This work, and related experiments with embryonic cells derived from regular mouse embryos, eventually helped Hayashi's team understand which genes would be needed to coax stem cells into becoming egg progenitor cells called primordial germ cells.

There was a catch: primordial germ cells, which can develop into either sperm or eggs, still have two sets of chromosomes like any typical animal cell. To form sex cells, which have just one set of genes from each parent, germ cells must twice undergo cell division in a process called meiosis. In females, the first cell division happens in the embryo as the primordial germ cell enters the reproductive system. The second division happens during ovulation when the egg is finally matured after exposure to a number of hormones. After creating the primordial germ cell, Hayashi and his co-workers were able to place them back into a live mouse to complete their development–reaching what was then the boundary of science. To create viable eggs in a dish, however, researchers would need to understand and re-create each step along the pathway to maturation.

The key, the scientists discovered, was to more carefully mimic nature. They spent several years tweaking the solution in which the converted egg cells were grown. One breakthrough came when the team added cells from ovaries of other mouse fetuses into the medium while they matured the cells in a dish. The ovaries released a mixture of hormones–basically creating an ovarylike environment to fool the cells into thinking they were in the body. Furthermore, the scientists altered the viscosity of the fluid medium to mimic what would be found in the mouse.

Once they got that medium right, and the eggs were matured in the lab, the next steps were akin to any other in vitro fertilization (IVF) procedure. The researchers first married the mature eggs and normal mouse sperm together in the lab. After a few days, they selected a promising embryo using a tiny pipette and injected it into a female mouse that would incubate the mouse fetus for 20 days. Finally, after many failed attempts in which the mouse would miscarry, or the embryo would not implant, or it would become stillborn, the process at last led to one healthy pup. Eventually more followed.

The process is still far from perfect, however. Only 16 of the hundreds of stem cells Hayashi's group created survived the five-week mouse-egg-maturation process. And when the scientists coupled the successful lab-made eggs with sperm, only an extremely small percentage of those skin-cells-turned-eggs went on to become healthy mouse pups (compared with a 62 percent success rate for eggs taken from adult mice and fertilized in vitro). Yet the scientists proved that their methods could work. Those eight pups grew up to be normal and healthy. They even went on to have mates and to birth lively pups of their own.

When Sperm Meets Egg

Plenty of people require reproductive help. More than 10 percent of American men and a similar percentage of women are considered infertile. Options for overcoming infertility are arduous and often unsuccessful. IVF, for example, requires a woman to undergo a week or two of hormone shots designed to release multiple eggs. A handful of those eggs will then be fertilized with sperm in a lab, and one or two will be implanted. The cost, largely paid out of pocket, can easily top $20,000, and yet approximately 65 percent of in vitro fertilization cycles still fail, often because of poor egg quality. Moreover, IVF cannot help if someone has no healthy eggs or sperm.

It is obvious why mining human blood or skin cells to make a baby is an alluring alternative. Instead of extracting human eggs, a health-care worker could draw a small vial of a potential mother's blood. (Blood, which is routinely drawn in medical facilities, might be easier to access in human patients than skin cells, Hayashi says, although either could be used.)

Scientists in a lab could transform those blood cells into stem cells and then, after a few more steps, into eggs or sperm. Next, the manufactured egg could be fertilized with normal sperm, or vice versa, and implanted into the woman using the same method as IVF–leaving the child with the same genetic inheritance they would normally get from each parent.

Hayashi says that right now the procedure is too risky to apply to humans and would become acceptable only if the eggs that scientists create can lead to healthy embryos as often as natural ones do. To begin with, researchers will have to show that they can keep the eggs alive in the lab long enough to closely emulate what would be necessary for human development. (In mice, egg cells mature in five days; in women, they require roughly 30.) Yet before reproductive scientists can even think about creating babies this way, they will have to confirm that the process will work in larger animals that more closely resemble people.

Growing Together

To overcome that hump, Hayashi's team is already working with primates: marmoset monkeys. But several major challenges have hindered its progress. Mice are good research subjects because they ovulate every five days and are pregnant for 20. Marmoset pregnancies last more than 140 days, so making a baby would take longer, even if all the science worked perfectly. It takes much longer for primordial germ cells in a marmoset to mature into eggs than it does for mouse eggs to mature, and Hayashi and his team have yet to find a lab environment that keeps the cells alive long enough for that to happen.

In their rodent work, the researchers learned how to mature primordial germ cells outside of living mice, but they still needed ovarian cells from mice fetuses to aid the process. To make sure the primordial germ cells survive and mature in monkeys—and to be able to scale up this work to ultimately create many more lab-grown eggs—Hayashi thinks he will have to do more than simply transfer ovarian cells to a lab dish. He will have to identify the specific ovarian cells that send key signals for maturation and figure out how to derive them from stem cells. That way, in future stages of the work, he would be able to grow all the necessary ingredients—rather than remain dependent on mining other fetuses for their ovarian cells.

Surani, director of germ-line and epigenomics research at Gurdon and a pioneer in this field, has been experimenting with different combinations of these key "helper" cells to support the germ cells' maturation and communication. "The [germ] cells actually go through to a certain point, and then they need something very specific to break through the next point—they need a change of signal or environment—or something," Surani explains. He and his team have been making educated guesses about which cells may be particularly significant in that process, but it is slow, painstaking work. To help guide their next steps, they are now studying aborted human fetuses for clues about each step of egg cell maturation. The lab has also started using pigs, instead of mice, because porcine development more closely resembles that of humans and because pigs are cheaper to work with than monkeys. Saitou and his lab recently published a paper in Science showing that they had created human egg precursor cells from adult cells. The process took a long time and yielded few egg-precursor-like structures, suggesting that making eggs in humans might be far more complicated than it was in mice.

Rather than tweaking lab dish protocols, there might be another way to further the process. Some researchers think they will get better results by moving their manufactured cells in vivo as soon as possible to piggyback off the body's natural quality-control systems that eliminate flawed gametes and leave more resources for the remaining cellular contenders. Renee Reijo Pera, a stem cell scientist at Montana State University, is taking that tack in her research with sperm. In nature, only the fittest sperm survive to fertilize the egg, but making and maturing sperm in a lab dish does away with that competition, increasing the risk that defective sperm will fertilize, she says. Because the human body is exquisitely tuned to weed out bad sperm, Reijo Pera focuses her work on making primordial sperm that can be matured in the testes. "We think the body should do the selecting," she says. "In a dish, I'm worried we'll force things to go forward that wouldn't in the natural environment."

No matter what precautions scientists take, some critics say artificial eggs or sperm should never be used to create human life. Marcy Darnovsky, for example, does not think that lab-generated germ cells could ever be safe enough to justify their risks. Darnovsky is executive director of the Center for Genetics and Society, a public-interest organization advocating for the responsible use of human genetic technologies. She says she fully supports research that leads to a better understanding of human and animal development. But she draws a line at using engineered eggs and sperm to generate a new life—especially a human one. "I think it's likely to be extremely biologically risky for any resulting children," she says, citing the example of mammalian cloning: many of the cloned embryos failed to develop, and some animals were born with terrible health problems. Darnovsky believes that public policy is needed to make sure that the scientific progress Hayashi, Surani, Reijo Pera, and others are pursuing does not go too far.

Other concerns persist about what this methodology might mean for our understanding of parenting. If anyone's cells could be manipulated into becoming sperm or egg, for example, could that portend a future where individuals' cells could become both sperm and egg–creating a uniparent? Or might someone be able to snatch up a stray skin cell from a person's napkin or bed to create a child without their consent or knowledge? Moreover, as George Daley, dean of Harvard Medical School, and his colleagues wrote in 2017 in *Science Translational Medicine*, such a technology could enable the creation of embryos on a previously unimagined scale–raising the specter of the devaluation of human life, as well as vexing policy challenges.

Ethical concerns have thus far constrained any human-related work on in vitro gametogenesis and have kept funding to a minimum, researchers say. Science involving embryos has long been restricted in the U.S. Whereas the Obama administration was friendlier to stem cell research than its predecessor, the pendulum has swung back somewhat under Donald Trump. In other countries as well, the lack of funding for such research and difficulty in accessing tissue samples of natural embryos for comparison add an extra layer of challenge to the research, according to Surani and Helen Picton, who does related work at the University of Leeds in England. Hayashi, for example, says it would be very difficult for him to do human germ-cell studies in his native Japan. (Japanese law forbids fertilizing human germ cells, even for research purposes.) But Jacob Hanna, a stem cell scientist at the Weizmann Institute of Science in Israel, says he has an easier time because of cultural interest in advancing reproductive technologies.

An Ethical Conundrum

Even if they never produce a human baby, though, scientists say simply pursuing the goal of making eggs and sperm will have payoffs: in treating infertility, understanding early development, and unraveling the effect that toxins can have on human inheritance. "It's a voyage of discovery," says Picton, who specializes in ovarian physiology and reproduction. Figuring out how to identify high-quality eggs and sperm may help improve the selection process for IVF, for example. And the process of refining the recipe for gamete creation will provide the first real insights into where cells go wrong to cause disease, birth defects, or cellular death.

Learning how to make eggs and sperm from skin or blood cells might also help scientists better unravel genetic inheritance known as epigenetics–changes not to the genes but to gene expression. Understanding how sperm and eggs are formed in their earliest days might allow us to scour those cells for any methyl groups or other changes that have accumulated in the genes. Right now questions abound regarding how some traits seem to get passed down without altering the underlying genetics. In a 2016 study, for instance, epigenetic changes to areas of genes associated with regulating stress hormones were found in the children of Holocaust survivors born years after their parents' trauma. The genes were unchanged, but how the genes acted seemed to get passed down. Being able to generate eggs and sperm from stem cells could allow scientists to dig into this epigenetic process, Surani says, and could offer insights into diseases of aging, which are often caused by the accumulation of epigenetic markers. Treatments for aging-related diseases might even come out of a new understanding of how these marks are erased in the developing germ cell.

Surani is now researching how mitochondria–the cells' energy source–perform during the egg-making process. Mitochondria go through a selection process during reproduction, with the child receiving only their mother's genetic material. The process of correcting defects in mitochondria is not well understood, but Surani hopes that by studying how the germ cell corrects such errors, he and his colleagues can learn a lot about cellular energy and related diseases. "Along the way, we can gather knowledge that could have a huge impact on human health," he says.

Hayashi hopes that such efforts will also be useful for rescuing and restoring nearly extinct species, such as the white rhinoceros. By improving their understanding of the process of forming gametes, researchers will be better poised to work with species that are likely to die out, he says. He is currently trying to reproduce his mouse research in northern white rhinos. Although progress is coming slowly, Hayashi thinks artificial insemination will eventually allow scientists to rescue the nearly extinct species. But the wait time is much longer. A mouse is pregnant for 20 days; a white rhino is pregnant for 16 months, he notes.

When Hayashi talks to audiences about his white rhino work, everyone looks happy, he says. But when he mentions doing similar research in humans, "some people are very skeptical, and some are very afraid." Hayashi understands their concerns. A lot of human germ cells and embryos would be wasted before human stem cells could successfully be transformed into viable eggs and sperm. Even the viable gametes might still carry the risk of birth defects, he cautions.

Reijo Pera believes that ethics do support studying this work for human applications—and, if it can be done safely enough, even using it to create humans. A cancer survivor who is infertile herself, Reijo Pera believes that helping couples have children justifies the quest.

Yet thorny questions remain about exactly what should be considered safe and who should decide that. When scientists developed other contentious technologies, such as IVF and the gene-editing CRISPR system, formal meetings among researchers, ethicists and members of the public helped to develop recommendations and guidelines for their potential applications. The same will likely be required for in vitro gametogenesis, researchers and ethicists note. Moreover, those conversations should take place long before the science is at a stage where humans can use it. "Before the inevitable, society will be well advised to strike and maintain a vigorous public conversation on the ethical challenges of [in vitro gametogenesis]," Daley and his colleagues wrote in their January 2017 paper. "With science and medicine hurtling forward at breakneck speed, the rapid transformation of reproductive and regenerative medicine may surprise us."

Referenced

Derivation of Oocytes from Mouse Embryonic Stem Cells. Karin Hübner et al. in *Science*, Vol. 300, pages 1251–1256; May 23, 2003.

Offspring from Oocytes Derived from In Vitro Primordial Germ Cell–Like Cells in Mice. Katsuhiko Hayashi et al. in *Science*, Vol. 338, pages 971–975; November 16, 2012.

Reconstitution In Vitro of the Entire Cycle of the Mouse Female Germ Line. Orie Hikabe et al. in *Nature*, Vol. 539, pages 299–303; November 10, 2016.

About the Author

Karen Weintraub is a staff writer at USA Today, *where she covers COVID, vaccine development and other health issues.*

Section 5: Policy and Politics

5.1 Abortion Pills Are Very Safe and Effective, yet Government Rules Still Hinder Access
By Claudia Wallis

5.2 Abortion Rights Are Good Health Care and Good Science
By The Editors of *Scientific American*

5.3 Being Denied an Abortion Has Lasting Impacts on Health and Finances
By Mariana Lenharo

5.4 To Prevent Women from Dying in Childbirth, First Stop Blaming Them
By Monica R. McLemore and Valentina D'Efilippo

5.5 Police Who Tear-Gas Abortion-Rights Protesters Could Induce Abortion
By Matthew R. Francis

Abortion Pills Are Very Safe and Effective, yet Government Rules Still Hinder Access

By Claudia Wallis

Ever since it was approved in 2000 as an abortion pill, mifepristone has been regulated as if it were a dangerous substance. The U.S. Food and Drug Administration required doctors to be specially certified to prescribe it. Patients had to sign an agreement confirming that they had been counseled on its risks. Most onerously, the pill had to be given in person in an approved clinical setting—even though a second drug used to complete the abortion, misoprostol, could be taken at home. In addition, 17 U.S. states have passed laws requiring an ultrasound scan before mifepristone can be prescribed. Yet decades of study have shown that the medication is safe and that those restrictions are needless, according to the American College of Obstetricians and Gynecologists and other medical groups. The rules have more to do with politics and ideology than with science.

It took the COVID pandemic to strip away the fig leaf of scientific justification from one regulation. The U.S. and several other countries that restrict mifepristone suspended the requirement of in-person distribution. Patients could access care via telemedicine and get the pills by mail rather than risk catching COVID at a clinic. A natural experiment unfolded that highlighted the safety of this approach. Last December the FDA acknowledged as much by permanently scrapping the in-person rule.

The agency did not, however, remove the other regulations. And although patients will be able to get their prescription at a drugstore or by mail, the FDA is requiring a new certification for pharmacies that dispense the drug. Such measures "continue to be necessary to ensure the benefits of mifepristone outweigh the risks," according to the FDA. Researchers who study medical abortion see this split decision as both a step forward and a missed opportunity at a time when abortion rights are in peril.

Mifepristone works by blocking progesterone, a hormone that maintains pregnancy. In a standard protocol, the drug is followed by a dose of misoprostol, which triggers contractions and expulsion of the embryo. "It is identical to how we often treat early miscarriage," notes Lesley Regan, who chairs the abortion task force of England's Royal College of Obstetricians and Gynecologists. In the U.S., the pills may be used during the first 10 weeks of gestation, although the World Health Organization considers them safe up to 12 weeks. Research confirms that medication abortion is about 95 percent effective in ending pregnancy. The risk of complications that require further medical attention–such as hemorrhage or infection–is less than 1 percent.

During the COVID era, at least three studies showed that the efficacy and safety hold up without in-person clinical visits. In fact, a large study done in the U.K.–where the government also provisionally allowed telehealth care–identified distinct advantages. It compared outcomes in more than 52,000 medication abortions during the two months before and after the government decision. Researchers found no increase in complications.

Moreover, the average wait time for treatment dropped from 10.7 days to 6.5 days, and 40 percent of abortions were completed at six weeks or earlier; only 25 percent met that mark with in-person drug treatment. Patient satisfaction was also higher with telemedicine, says the study's lead author, Abigail Aiken, an expert in reproductive health policy at the University of Texas at Austin. One reason is that people can be treated sooner: "When someone is facing a pregnancy that they didn't want, the mental stress and anxiety take a toll." Telemedicine is also more convenient and less expensive. Regan notes that it takes fewer health-care resources and better serves people who live far from an abortion clinic.

The U.K. study, along with two done in the U.S., also showed that an ultrasound scan is unnecessary except when patients report issues that warrant it, such as symptoms of an ectopic pregnancy (one outside the uterus), or if they cannot recall the date of their last menstrual period. Research shows that the date suffices to determine gestational age before abortion.

Ironically the FDA's sensible move on telemedicine is likely to widen state-by-state inequities in access to abortion. In most states access will improve. But 19 have laws mandating in-person abortion care, and "six specifically ban mailing the pills," notes Elizabeth Nash of the Guttmacher Institute. Further restrictions are probable in abortion-hostile states if the U.S. Supreme Court fails to protect abortion rights later this year, as is widely expected. Aiken predicts that "we're going to see this picture of uneven access–this zip code lottery–diverge even further."

About the Author

Claudia Wallis is an award-winning science journalist whose work has appeared in the New York Times, Time, Fortune *and the* New Republic. *She was science editor at* Time *and managing editor of* Scientific American Mind.

Abortion Rights Are Good Health Care and Good Science

By The Editors of Scientific American

The U.S. Supreme Court is about to make a huge mistake.

If the leaked draft opinion in *Dobbs v. Jackson Women's Health Organization* is a true indication of the court's will, federal abortion rights in this country are about to be struck down. In doing so the court will not only side against popular opinion on a crucial issue of bodily autonomy, but also signal that politics and religion play a more important role in health care than do science and evidence.

For almost 50 years people in the U.S. who have needed to end a pregnancy have had a legal right to do so. Accessibility and affordability have always been barriers, and anti-abortion lawmakers have chipped away at this right, set forth in *Roe v. Wade*, but the ability to get a safe and legal abortion before fetal viability was settled law.

The new decision would strike down *Roe* and *Planned Parenthood v. Casey*, an opinion that overturned a Pennsylvania law that required a pregnant married woman to notify her husband in order to obtain abortion services. Many states, mainly governed by conservative lawmakers, have already passed or are planning to introduce laws that either ban abortion outright or put such severe restrictions on this medical procedure that it will be practically impossible to legally end a pregnancy. Some states will make criminals of doctors and other health-care providers who perform abortions. Some laws set to go into effect after a Supreme Court ruling would deny people the right to end pregnancies that happen after rape or incest or that pose grave medical dangers. These laws are contrary to all relevant science, and any health-related claims used to support them are demonstrably wrong.

In passing these laws, anti-abortion legislators often claim that abortion harms people who are pregnant. In a landmark study from the University of California, San Francisco, scientists found the opposite: denying people abortions led to worse mental and physical health, as well as financial stability. The Turnaway Study looked at about 1,000 women who were seeking abortions and followed them for five years. Some were just early enough in their pregnancies that they got the procedure, and others were turned away because their pregnancies were slightly past the legal cutoff where they lived. Women who had abortions reported fewer mental health issues, even years later, and their most common reaction was relief. Women denied abortions often experienced brief declines in mental health and higher anxiety.

Women denied abortions were more likely to end up poor, unemployed, or receiving government assistance, even though before they asked for an abortion they were in a similar financial place as women who were able to get one. This study, and others, tell us what will happen in a post-*Roe* world, when people are forced to carry unwanted pregnancies to term because they are denied a most basic form of health care and the ability to make decisions about their own bodies. Access to abortion largely appears to have very positive effects on people's lives.

The fight against abortion rights is often depicted as a religious mission, but not all religions or religious believers oppose abortion. We note that these political moves are part of a long-standing effort by some conservative Christians, as well as anti-abortion politicians and activists.

By forcing people to have children when they don't want to, these ideologues strip women of political and earning power, in some cases making them dependent upon men. By forcing people to have children when they are not financially secure, these laws prolong patterns of poverty. And the states with the most restrictive abortion policies often have the worst social safety nets, the worst maternal mortality rates, and the greatest health-care inequities.

This ideology denies the dangers of pregnancy, despite the fact that in some U.S. states maternal mortality approaches that of some developing nations. Some of the abortion restrictions states have passed are pegged to an early stage of pregnancy. But the biological and genetic problems that lead to complications with pregnancy are too numerous to list, and too variable from person to person to assign a deadline to. Gestational age cutoffs, "heartbeat" laws, and total bans go against the basic workings of human biology.

Regardless of how they legally justify their ruling, the justices of the Supreme Court who choose to strike down abortion rights are telling the American public that science doesn't matter, that evidence can be ignored. High courts have similarly said as much in striking down mask and vaccine mandates during the COVID pandemic. The logic of Alito's draft–the right to an abortion is not in the Constitution–could apply to all reproductive health, including the *Griswold v. Connecticut* Supreme Court decision that overturned a law banning birth control. The highest court in the land must value evidence and respect best medical practices, and yet the conservative majority clearly doesn't.

President Joe Biden and other pro-choice elected officials have said they will work to protect abortion rights. There are legislative means to ensure some degree of abortion access. But with our current federal legislature and the filibuster in place, getting the needed votes to pass measures protecting abortion will be difficult, if not impossible. We hope lawmakers will see abortion rights as an issue that makes it necessary to break through legislative roadblocks.

As our Supreme Court is poised to radically constrain the lives of so many people in the U.S, we applaud those states that are strengthening their abortion protections. We applaud those people who are continuing to fight the legal and practical battles for our right to health care and our right to privacy. And we applaud the health care workers–the doctors, the nurses, the medical assistants–and the volunteers, donors, and programs that help people who are pregnant care for themselves and their health. Safe and accessible reproductive health care is a basic right that is supported by science, medicine, and respect for human dignity. Everyone should have access to it.

Being Denied an Abortion Has Lasting Impacts on Health and Finances

By Mariana Lenharo

As the Supreme Court decides the future of abortion laws in the U.S., a key question to be considered is whether access to the procedure has positive or negative consequences for the people who get an abortion, and for society in general.

Dobbs v. Jackson Women's Health Organization concerns the constitutionality of a new Mississippi law that would ban abortions after 15 weeks of pregnancy. The case challenges the Supreme Court's 1973 *Roe v. Wade* decision, a precedent that protects abortion access before fetal viability—a point at around 24 weeks of gestation, when a fetus is considered able to survive outside the uterus.

Antiabortion activists often contend that abortion harms women physically and psychologically. Another argument, made by Mississippi Attorney General Lynn Fitch, is that there are now many laws that protect equal economic opportunity—suggesting that abortion access is no longer necessary to help women pursue financial independence.

Examining the validity of these claims has been notoriously difficult. The most scientific way to measure how getting an abortion impacts a pregnant person would be through a randomized controlled trial—which would require the obviously impossible scenario of people who seek an abortion being designated by researchers to either receive one or not. "The challenge is: we cannot feasibly or ethically randomly assign abortion access to people to measure what happens to their lives," says Caitlin Myers, a professor of economics at Middlebury College.

Thus, until recently, the few studies that tried to measure the impacts of abortion access had an important limitation. They compared groups that were too different to begin with—for example, people who got abortions and people who chose to give birth.

But one study has made great progress in measuring the impact of abortion access. To address the methodological limitations in previous studies, researcher Diana Greene Foster, a professor in the department of obstetrics, gynecology, and reproductive sciences at the University of California, San Francisco, designed a novel approach. Her team recruited women at abortion clinics, and compared outcomes among those who were just over the gestational limit and were denied an abortion with those who were just under the limit and had the procedure. Foster called the investigation the Turnaway Study, a reference to clinics turning some people away because they are too far along in their pregnancy. Its results have been described in 50 scientific papers, almost all of which were published in peer-reviewed journals from 2012 to 2020. And to date, the study is one of the most comprehensive in the field.

"The real innovation of the Turnaway Study," Foster says, "was to take people who received an abortion and compare them to [those who had] the only other outcome that is available to somebody who is pregnant and doesn't want to be—which is to carry that pregnancy to term."

From 2008 to 2010 the study recruited nearly 1,000 women seeking abortions at 30 facilities in 21 states. Afterward the participants were interviewed by phone every six months for a span of five years. (While transgender men and nonbinary people also experience pregnancy and seek abortions, the Turnaway Study focused specifically on pregnant women.) The study found that, compared with women who received an abortion, those who wanted the procedure but were denied it fared worse in numerous aspects of their life, including financial situation, education, and physical and mental health.

Because of how it was able to isolate the effect of abortion access in a natural experiment, the Turnaway Study is recognized by the scientific community as an important contribution to the field, generating data that many scientists say should be considered by policy makers. "The rigid cutoff generates a situation where you've got women immediately on either side of the cutoff being extremely similar in characteristics and circumstances—but one can have an abortion and the other one can't," says Phillip Levine, a Wellesley College professor of economics, who was not involved with the study. "The Turnaway Study has the advantage of providing information that would otherwise be very difficult to ascertain regarding the impact of an abortion on women."

"It's impossible to overstate how scholarly the design of the study is," says Amanda Stevenson, an assistant professor of sociology at the University of Colorado Boulder, who was also not involved with the investigation. She says that the researchers cleverly drew from their knowledge of how abortion care delivery happens in the U.S. to find a natural experiment that answered their questions.

Poverty and Unemployment

When it comes to the socioeconomic implications of abortion access, the Turnaway Study found that women who were denied the procedure and carried the pregnancy to term were more likely to live in poverty. Six months after they sought an abortion, 61 percent of them were below the U.S. federal poverty level, compared with 45 percent among the group who received an abortion just under the limit. And at the same point, people in the former group were also more likely to be unemployed (51 percent versus 37 percent among women who had an abortion) and to receive financial benefits from the Temporary Assistance for Needy Families (TANF) program (more than 15 percent versus less than 8 percent). Between one and five years after seeking an abortion, women who were denied the procedure and ended up giving birth were more likely to report not having enough money to cover living expenses, a more subjective poverty measure.

Myers, who was not involved with the work and whose research focuses on the effects of reproductive policies, says she was initially a bit skeptical about the study's design. "I thought that there still could be something different about the people who showed up a little too late–that they might unobservably have other factors in their lives that were causing them to show up a little bit too late that were also causing them to have different outcomes," she says.

For Myers, what put those concerns to rest was seeing a subsequent analysis, also a part of the Turnaway Study, in which researchers linked the study's participants to their credit scores. "What I found so powerful was that they [the authors] don't just match them at the time they seek the abortion. They match them for an extensive time period prior to experiencing the unintended pregnancy," Myers says. "And they show that their financial circumstances are trending very similarly right up until the moment that they go to the abortion providers and experience different outcomes."

The credit score analysis was led by Sarah Miller, an assistant professor of business economics and public policy at the University of Michigan, who had the idea after seeing the Turnaway Study's initial socioeconomic findings. Her work shows that women who were denied an abortion suffered an increase in financial distress that lasted several years. And these women's debt increased by 78 percent, compared with their average prebirth debt. Their number of negative public records, such as bankruptcy and eviction, increased by 81 percent, also compared with their prebirth average.

"What this study has done is that it has very convincingly shown that being denied an abortion has these economic effects," says Jason Lindo, a professor of economics at Texas A&M University, who provided feedback for the credit score paper but was not directly involved in the work. He notes that the findings are consistent with the broader scientific literature, which indicates that having children in general can lead to negative economic consequences.

Health and Emotions

One of the key questions that Foster was looking to answer when she designed the Turnaway Study was: Does abortion hurt women? The investigation found that, in the long term, more women who gave birth (27 percent) reported fair or poor physical health, compared with women who had an abortion (20 percent for a first-trimester abortion and 21 percent for second-trimester one). "The biggest differences we saw, besides the socioeconomic differences, are in physical health," Foster says. "That's consistent with the medical literature that shows that carrying a pregnancy to term–the many months of continued pregnancy and childbirth–are associated with much greater risk than having an abortion, even a later abortion."

Two women in the Turnaway Study died from childbirth; there were no abortion-related deaths. Stevenson notes that, while the investigation was not designed to study mortality, two pregnancy-related deaths are more than what would be normally expected for a population of that size. "What that tells us is that it is quite possible that people who are seeking abortion care, right on the edge of when abortion is currently available in most places, are at elevated risk of pregnancy-related mortality," she says. "This is not conclusive evidence because that was not the intention of the study. But it is a very surprising finding."

When it comes to the participants' mental health, the study found no evidence of harm from having an abortion. "There were no emergent cases of depression, anxiety, or suicidality," Foster says. What she and her colleagues did find was a short-term decline in mental health among those who were denied an abortion, with increased self-reported anxiety symptoms and lower self-esteem and life satisfaction.

Prior studies suggest that women seeking an abortion tend to have more existing mental health disorders than women who choose to carry their pregnancy to term. "It explains why we see a correlation or association between abortion and subsequent mental health in some data," says Julia Steinberg, an associate professor at the department of family science at the University of Maryland School of Public Health.

Correlation is not necessarily causation, as statisticians often note. Epidemiologist Chelsea Polis, a researcher in the department of epidemiology at the Johns Hopkins Bloomberg School of Public

Health, and her colleagues did a systematic review of studies looking into long-term mental health outcomes potentially related to abortion. They found that higher-quality studies reported no significant differences in long-term mental health between women who choose to abort a pregnancy and those who do not. "We also found that the opposite holds true for studies with the weakest research methodologies: those studies consistently found negative mental effects from abortion," Polis says.

The Turnaway Study found no evidence of emerging negative emotions five years after an abortion among the participants who had access to the procedure. In fact, relief was the predominant emotion reported at all times during the study. Additionally, at each data collection point throughout the five years, 95 percent of these women reported that having an abortion was the right decision.

What the data show, Foster says, is that women who seek an abortion understand the consequences of carrying a pregnancy to term and make a decision that reflects the outcomes they are likely to experience if they are unable to end the pregnancy. "They say that they don't have the money to support a child, and we see that their economic outcomes suffer. They say that their relationship isn't strong enough to raise a child, and we see that their relationship deteriorates. They say that they want to pursue other life outcomes, and we see that those life outcomes are strongly affected by whether they are able to get their abortion."

Foster says she is now setting up a new study to document the potential impact of the end of *Roe* in the U.S. "It seems very likely that our Supreme Court will allow 15-week bans or allow states to ban abortion entirely," she says. "Either way, I am designing a study to recruit people served just before the law was implemented and those who were turned away just after." Foster adds that she is also working with scientists in Nepal to study the effect of abortion receipt and denial in a context with high maternal mortality, widespread unsafe abortions, and high malnutrition among children.

Consequences of Stricter Abortion Laws

Scientists caution that the Turnaway Study looked at a specific group of women: those who sought an abortion relatively late in their pregnancy. More than 90 percent of women who seek the procedure in the U.S. do so within the first 13 weeks of gestation. "My guess, based on the evidence, is that the results would likely be the same with an earlier cutoff if there were such experiments," Levine says. "But it's also important to recognize that we don't necessarily know that."

Even if a direct extrapolation is not possible, the Turnaway findings hint at what could happen if the Supreme Court allows states to ban or further restrict abortion, according to Liza Fuentes, a senior research scientist at the Guttmacher Institute. "It gives us insight into the types of negative outcomes that we could expect for people–if they are unable to travel, to obtain an abortion–living in a state that makes abortion unavailable," says Fuentes, who was not involved with the study.

Myers notes that one of the pillars of Mississippi's argument for overturning *Roe* is that access to abortion has made little difference in people's lives. "That is patently false," she says. "We have solid scientific evidence showing that *Roe* mattered to people's lives, and we know that abortion access matters to people's lives now. And that is where I think it's very important for science to come in and say, 'We have answers to these questions of fact.'"

About the Author

Mariana Lenharo is a science and health journalist with a master's in journalism from Columbia University.

To Prevent Women from Dying in Childbirth, First Stop Blaming Them

By Monica R. McLemore and Valentina D'Efilippo

The shameful secret is out: Although the number of women who die in childbirth globally has fallen in recent decades, the rates in the U.S. have gone up. Since 1987 maternal mortality has doubled in the U.S. Now approximately 800 maternal deaths occur every year. One of the most striking takeaways from examining the data is racial disparity: Black women are three to four times more likely to die from pregnancy-related conditions such as cardiac issues and hemorrhage and to bear the brunt of serious complications. That risk is equally shared by all Black women regardless of income, education, or geographical location. In other words, the factors that typically protect people during pregnancy are not protective for Black women.

Fortunately, most of these deaths are considered preventable, and therefore much more can be done to stop them. First, everyone—from doctors to the media to the public—needs to stop blaming women for their own deaths. Instead we should focus on better understanding the underlying contributing factors. These include a lack of data, not educating patients about signs and symptoms—and not believing them when they speak up, errors made by health-care providers, and poor communication among different health-care teams. Finally, studies have shown that interventions such as wider access to midwifery, group prenatal care, and social and doula support are effective in improving maternal health outcomes.

Progress has been slow and uneven. Deaths from hemorrhage, for example, have been reduced by half in some states because of standardized tool kits for care. And California has led in the pursuit of understanding root causes of maternal mortality. Still, structural racism is proving to be an intractable force.

The U.S. Is an Outlier

The high maternal mortality rate (MMR) in the U.S. is often blamed on the poor health of mothers, but a comparison with other wealthy countries undermines this argument. MMR–shown here using two estimates, one by the World Health Organization (WHO) and one by the Institute for Health Metrics and Evaluation (IHME)–is not rising in countries with similarly increased rates of cardiovascular disease, obesity, diabetes, and other conditions during pregnancy. Different factors must therefore be contributing to the rise in MMR in the U.S. As a 2018 paper in *Obstetrics & Gynecology* concluded, "the increased mortality ratios seen in the United States in recent years reflect significant social as well as medical challenges and are closely related to lack of access to health care in the non-Hispanic Black population.

Maternal Mortality Data in the U.S. Are an Unreliable Mess

As bad as the numbers sound, the U.S. MMR is widely considered to be an underestimate. That is because different methods are used to count deaths related to pregnancy, and reporting is inconsistent. The World Health Organization, for instance, defines maternal death as the death of a woman while pregnant or within 42 days of the end of a pregnancy. But the Centers for Disease Control and Prevention defines maternal mortality as "the death of a woman while pregnant or within one year of the end of a pregnancy." Both definitions exclude accidental or incidental causes of death. The difference in time frame for maternal mortality is further complicated at the state level, where data collection from death certificates is not comparable because of different definitions of the cause and time of death. States could fix this problem by creating standardized maternal mortality review committees that comprehensively evaluate each maternal death and discuss the factors that contributed to the outcome.

Who Is Dying?

It's common to blame women for their own deaths. Many scientific publications have cited that women are coming to pregnancy older (called advanced maternal age, or geriatric pregnancy), sicker (with hypertension, diabetes, or other chronic illnesses), and fatter (that is, with obesity). But even in studies that control for age, chronic disease and obesity, the MMR in the U.S. still far exceeds rates in similarly wealthy nations. In a 2016 report that looked at pregnancy-related death disparities among states, the authors wrote that "excellent care is apparently available but is not reaching all the people."

Why Are Mothers Dying—And How Many Causes Are Preventable?

Pregnancy exacerbates existing clinical conditions such as cardiovascular disease (including high blood pressure), enlarged heart, and an irregular heartbeat. Black women are more likely to have these conditions before, during, and after pregnancy. Chronic toxic stress–the way that experiences of discrimination are embodied–has been shown to make these conditions worse. But in the U.K., for example, there were only two deaths from preeclampsia and eclampsia over a three-year period, according to a 2018 study, suggesting deaths from these hypertensive disorders of pregnancy are highly preventable. Life-threatening heavy bleeding, or hemorrhage, is also one of the major risk factors for death and is easily preventable. One way this can be done is to develop checklists that document bleeding over time and interventions to address it; these checklists must be accessible to all members of a health-care team.

How the U.S. Is Tackling the Problem—Or Not

Several groups, including the World Health Organization, have called for a more respectful approach to maternal care. This would be helped by diversification of the health-care workforce so that clinical teams reflect the populations they serve. It also means better communication of knowledge between patients and their health-care teams. One program that embraces these features is called the Alliance for Innovation on Maternal Health (AIM). Funded through the federal Maternal and Child Health Bureau, AIM is a national alliance to promote consistent and safe maternity care. It launched with the initial goal of reducing maternal mortality by 1,000 instances–and severe maternal morbidity by 100,000 instances–between 2014 and 2018. Many states are currently participating. The efforts involved in AIM include hospital-based interventions whereby health-care teams–from obstetricians to emergency room staff–practice simulations of emergencies. The alliance also advocates for increased access to doulas and midwives, as well as a reclamation of normal physiological birth–that is, not treating birth as a disease to be managed.

California Leads the Way

Established in 2006, the California Maternal Quality Care Collaborative (CMQCC) set out to use data-driven approaches to understand the root causes of maternal mortality. A few of their tactics included distributing plain-language tool kits, conducting mock emergencies, making quality improvements in hospital settings and training staff to work more collaboratively. Despite admirable reductions in overall maternal mortality in California, significant racial disparities remain and align with the demographics represented in the national data sets. Keeping Black women alive before, during, and after birth was the focus of an innovative hospital-based racial equity pilot program: the SACRED Birth study, launched in 2020 by University of California, San Francisco, associate professor of obstetrics Karen A. Scott. This community-centered study co-led by Black women and community-based organizations provides essential insights on achieving birth equity and justice. Data collection ended at the beginning of 2021.

About the Authors

Monica R. McLemore is an associate professor in the Family Health Care Nursing Department and a clinician-scientist at Advancing New Standards in Reproductive Health at the University of California, San Francisco.

Valentina D'Efilippo is an award-winning designer, creative director, and co-author of The Infographic History of the World. *A voice in the field of data design, she leads a series of Masterclasses with the* Guardian.

Police Who Tear-Gas Abortion-Rights Protesters Could Induce Abortion

By Matthew R. Francis

After the recent ruling by the Supreme Court overturning federal abortion rights, people have taken to the streets in protest. In multiple places, police attacked protesters with chemical weapons in the form of tear gas. In Arizona, law enforcement even fired canisters from the windows of government buildings.

One irony inherent in this violence is that chemical weapons can cause spontaneous abortions, commonly known as miscarriages. In other words, law enforcement officers use dangerous, unregulated weapons against unarmed civilians, possibly violating protesters' human rights by terminating pregnancies that, according to the Supreme Court, those same protesters have no constitutionally protected right to terminate themselves.

Researchers elsewhere in the world have identified associations between chemical weapons and miscarriage. United Nations observers recorded miscarriages after Israeli police used tear gas on Palestinian civilians during the 1988 uprisings, leading to stricter rules on when the weapons should be used. Toxicology researchers led by Andrei Tchernitchin of the University of Chile found enough evidence linking spontaneous abortion and a type of tear gas to convince the Chilean government to suspend tear gas use in 2011. And the Nobel Peace Prize–winning organization Physicians for Human Rights argued in 2012 that Bahrain had violated U.N. guidelines on chemical weapons use, based in part on increased miscarriages.

These weapons should not be used on anyone under any circumstances. The 1925 Geneva Protocol was intended to ban military use of chemical weapons in warfare. However, the relevant treaties don't extend to nations using such weapons on their own people. That means police and other government forces are free to tear-gas unarmed civilians in the name of law enforcement, while soldiers could be prosecuted for war crimes if they did the same to armed combatants.

It is essentially legal for police to endanger pregnancies by assaulting protesters with likely abortifacients.

Tear gas is a euphemistic name for several crowd-control (another euphemism) chemicals containing chlorine, including CS (o-chlorobenzylidene malononitrile), CR (dibenzoxazepine), CX (phosgene oxime), and CN (chloroacetophenone). While all these compounds do cause the eyes to produces tears, they primarily activate pain receptors, as well as making victims vomit and cough. Police claim they use these chemical weapons on crowds to disperse them, but the physical results often include disorientation, panic, and respiratory problems.

The most widely used tear gas is CS, from the initials of its discoverers Ben Corson and Roger Stoughton, who created it in 1928. Notoriously, the U.S. Army exposed volunteers from the ranks of soldiers to increasingly larger concentrations and gauged their responses, a test that led the CDC to declare CS "immediately dangerous to life or health." Other than that (arguably unethical) experiment, chemical weapons have mostly been used on the general public without testing to determine the harm it might cause to anyone who isn't an able-bodied young cisgender man.

While researchers and human rights organizations are clear on the connection between tear gas and miscarriage, how it works is much harder to identify.

"Tear gas has so many components that any one of them could potentially cause fetal harm," says Rohini Haar, who is a medical doctor with Physicians for Human Rights and a faculty member at the University of California, Berkeley. "Dissecting the impact of tear gas from the many confounders is going to be challenging—stress, mental health issues, impacts of arrest, and other canister components other than the CS compound is near impossible."

In other words, the chemical component CS itself may not be causing miscarriage, but tear gas is so demonstrably harmful to physical and mental health that it hardly matters from a human rights perspective. A weapon that stresses a person's body or mind so much that they spontaneously abort is not better in any way than a chemical that does the same thing via a more direct biochemical process.

Nor is it ethical to test chemical weapons on pregnant people in the lab, adds Haar: "A randomized controlled trial is not possible here. To put it in perspective, I'm not sure we need hard 'proof' that this is a huge problem of tear gas itself causing miscarriages–there are lots of reasons we need to regulate and limit it, this concern among them."

The U.S. government does not regulate the use of chemical weapons on its own people. Even senators have criticized the lack of available information on the use of tear gas, particularly the many issues with its safety.

That lack of regulation means that, in some instances, police have been buying increasingly strong chemical weapons to use on crowds. The Chemical Weapons Research Group in Portland, Oregon, documented many types of weapons used during the 2020 uprisings over police brutality in the United States, which included military-grade smoke grenades and versions of tear gas containing powdered oleoresin capsicum (OC, the same ingredient as pepper sprays, marketed by some companies as "panic powder"). These increased-strength weapons have not been documented in protests prior to 2020.

These compounds may be disruptive to endocrine processes and reproductive organs. Protestors reported irregular and disrupted menstruation after police gassed them.

As New York Representative Alexandria Ocasio-Cortez pointed out on Twitter, "Forced pregnancy is a crime against humanity." Forced abortion is also a crime against humanity, as established by the U.N. People have already been arrested for having miscarriages, which raises serious concern that police or prosecutors may blame a protestor if tear gas causes their miscarriage. The policy of "qualified immunity" protects police from lawsuits alleging excessive force and other forms of violence, meaning someone who loses their pregnancy due to tear gas may not have any legal recourse.

The police reaction to protests following police murders of George Floyd, Michael Brown, Breonna Taylor, and other Black people also highlights that chemical, abortifacient weapons are used discriminately against Black protesters.

To be clear, chemical weapons would violate human rights even if they didn't cause miscarriages, and pregnant people have a constitutionally protected right to participate in protests. The same politicians and justices who call themselves "pro-life" are happy to sanction police violence against protesters, to the point where that violence could end pregnancies. Coerced abortion is just as much a violation of human rights as forced birth or involuntary pregnancy, even—perhaps especially—when carried out in the name of the law.

The author would like to thank Kathryn Clancy of the University of Illinois at Urbana-Champaign for her help with the biochemical literature on chemical weapons effects.

This is an opinion and analysis article, and the views expressed by the author or authors are not necessarily those of Scientific American.

About the Author

Matthew R. Francis is a science writer, journalist, physicist, and frequent wearer of dapper hats. A former college professor who also directed a planetarium, he has written about everything from cosmology to mathematical biology to social justice issues in science.

Section 6: *Roe* v. *Dobbs*

Abortion Restrictions Could Cause an Ob-Gyn Brain Drain

By Monique Brouillette

Lisa Harris, an ob-gyn and researcher at the University of Michigan, recalls being paged to the operating room late on a Friday night to treat a pregnant woman who was hemorrhaging uncontrollably. The patient had been undergoing a procedure to treat a complication involving too much amniotic fluid in the uterus, and things went awry. In Harris's experience, she says, "performing an abortion within minutes or hours can be lifesaving in this situation."

Harris was the only one in the hospital that night who had been trained in abortion care. She performed a procedure called a dilation and evacuation (D&E), which dilates the cervix and empties the uterus. It is routinely used for abortion during the second trimester. Harris believes it is also the best way to treat a hemorrhage because it is safe, mostly painless, and minimally invasive.

She fears that if she had not been there, her patient would have ended up having a hysterotomy, a procedure in which a doctor cuts into the abdomen to remove the contents of the uterus (not to be confused with a hysterectomy, which is removal of the uterus). In this case, the fetus was too early to be viable, so it would not survive. More physicians know how to perform a hysterotomy than a D&E, and when faced with an emergency, the former procedure might have been the only option for them. But cutting into the uterus at an early stage of pregnancy can cause complications in future pregnancies.

Abortion skills are "emergency lifesaving skills," Harris says. And she worries that the Supreme Court's decision to overturn *Roe v. Wade* will have dire consequences not only for pregnant people but also for the doctors who care for them. For the first time in 50 years, many obstetricians will lose their ability to provide their patients with an important type of evidence-based medical care. The shift could send ripple effects through the field for generations.

Aborted Education

According to a study published in the April 2022 issue of *Obstetrics & Gynecology*, 128 of the 286 ob-gyn residency programs in the U.S. are located in the 26 states that either had "trigger laws" already in place to restrict abortion or are likely to restrict it. This means that roughly 45 percent of these programs will no longer offer training in abortion skills–which are also miscarriage skills, according to Harris and many others.

"I worry that when we take abortion training away from ob-gyn residents, we will take away an entire skill set that is useful not only for abortion care but [also] for miscarriage management," says the study's lead author Kavita Vinekar, an ob-gyn and researcher at the University of California, Los Angeles's David Geffen School of Medicine. With roughly half of the nation's training programs set to be affected by the bans, it is unlikely that providers will be able to travel out of state for proper training. Available programs simply will not have the capacity. "There will be an entire generation of physicians who will be ill-equipped to manage some of the most common and acute things that we see," Vinekar says.

Of all the non-abortion-care complications during pregnancy, miscarriage management is likely to be impacted most. And with roughly 10 to 20 percent of all known pregnancies ending in miscarriage, this will affect a considerable number of patients. Iffath Hoskins, president of the American College of Obstetricians and Gynecologists (ACOG), said in a recent press conference that "it is going to be very difficult for us clinicians to manage" this complication. Helping treat a patient's miscarriage may put them in a difficult position with the law because doing so may be seen as crossing the line into abortion. According to Hoskins, physicians may need to get another clinical opinion–or even legal counsel–before proceeding with treatment.

"It's going to have a devastating effect on every aspect of a woman's health care," she said.

Jennifer Kerns, an ob-gyn at the University of California, San Francisco, has seen the effects of this firsthand. About once a month she travels to an abortion clinic that treats people from Texas. The state has been under abortion restrictions since a bill called SB 8, a law that bans abortions past the sixth week of pregnancy, was passed last year. Kerns says that people have been showing up with ectopic pregnancies that doctors in Texas have refused to treat. An ectopic pregnancy occurs when the embryo implants outside of the uterus. The embryo cannot survive, and the pregnant person will almost certainly miscarry, which risks bursting a fallopian tube. Yet there are individuals who have not been able to receive treatment for the condition since the six-week ban went into effect. "It's really sobering and concerning to think that we're delaying care for people," Kerns says.

A Health-Care Desert

Hampering an entire profession with restrictions that have nothing to do with medicine and affect the way its members care for their patients almost certainly impact the field for years to come, according to Deborah Bartz, an ob-gyn at Brigham and Women's Hospital in Boston. Many of her trainees are deliberately planning to avoid practicing in states that have abortion restrictions in place.

Comprehensive training in women's and pregnant people's health care is a priority for future physicians looking to practice obstetrics and gynecology, and Bartz fears many of them will avoid states in which such training is not offered. "These restrictive abortion laws could actually drain the physician workforce within those states," she says.

A survey of ob-gyn residents conducted in 2020 found that trainees were more likely to be satisfied with abortion training in their program if it was given routinely rather than optionally–or not at all. Vinekar echoes the importance of the procedure. "As a physician who's a practicing ob-gyn, I want to take the best possible care of my patients," she says. "I would never take a job that didn't let me provide abortion care."

About the Author

Monique Brouillette is a freelance journalist who covers biology.

Genetic Counselors Scramble Post-*Roe* to Provide Routine Pregnancy Services without Being Accused of a Crime

By Laura Hercher

The June 24 decision by the Supreme Court to overturn *Roe v. Wade* struck close to home for genetic counselors, the medical professionals who are often tasked with advising and consoling prospective parents when ultrasounds or other prenatal tests indicate a threat to their own health or the health of their future child. People seeking abortions based on health concerns during pregnancy are a small percentage of abortion seekers overall, but they are disproportionately affected by the new barrage of restrictions because detecting and confirming a prenatal diagnosis takes time. The abortion drug mifepristone is approved for use by the Food and Drug Administration only through the 10th week of pregnancy–well before patients receive the results of genetic testing or anatomy scans. Patients are also likely to find themselves in a bind because of state restrictions on how far along a pregnancy can be when an abortion takes place.

Prenatal counselors must now work around the need for patients to travel out of state for abortion care–and somehow try to help patients without the financial means to make these trips. The disparity of access is likely to exacerbate existing health risks associated with being poor and pregnant. "I'm very worried about maternal mortality," says genetic counselor Shannon Barringer. She has worked for 25 years in the state of Arkansas, where a trigger law that went into effect on June 24 has made abortion illegal even in cases where the fetus is not expected to survive. Barringer also worries that new legislation may make it harder for her to provide that help. "I know [legislators are] already working with national organizations to draft language that may interfere with health providers being able to refer out of state," she says.

In fact, existing and proposed laws restricting abortion have become so extreme that they are likely to affect all prenatal patients, not just those who need an abortion. In a recent series of interviews conducted by two graduate students at Sarah Lawrence College, prenatal genetic counselors practicing in states hostile to abortion said that the need to send patients out of state if they were to need an abortion created time pressure that affected many aspects of prenatal care. (The author of this article teaches at Sarah Lawrence.) Some counselors reported that they were rescheduling detailed anatomy scans, typically done between the 20th and 22nd week of pregnancy, to be carried out at 18 or even 16 weeks, despite evidence that earlier scans will miss some fetal anomalies and give less definitive information on others.

A fuller picture of the effect on genetic counseling can be seen in Texas, where these services have operated in a de facto post-*Roe* world since September 2021, when a law went into effect making all but the earliest abortions illegal. That same law also permits any citizen so inclined to sue anyone "aiding or abetting" an illegal abortion for a sum up to $10,000. While few of these vigilante suits have reached the courts, the law has succeeded in creating an atmosphere of fear and suspicion. In fact, all four genetic counselors from Texas interviewed by *Scientific American* for this article said that their institutions required them to speak anonymously. "I've tried consciously, since the law passed, to make the counseling session a safe place for people to go," says one counselor working in Houston. "But on the flip side of that, I wonder if I or my genetic counseling colleagues are opening ourselves up for potential lawsuits."

This tension between optimal patient care and self-preservation is not likely to improve anytime soon. New proposals directly target the ability of health professionals to provide guidance to their patients. A bill recently introduced in the South Carolina legislature would make it a felony, with mandatory prison time, to offer information to anyone attempting to obtain an abortion, even if one only directs that person to a website. With the threat of legal jeopardy, some genetic counselors may be deterred from even engaging in routine conversations that help determine which types of prenatal tests are best for an individual patient because they could be perceived as raising the question of whether or not that patient wants the option of terminating a pregnancy.

Concerns about liability have also raised questions about whether to limit what information goes into a medical record. "We've debated it," says another Houston counselor. "Certain people in our department feel strongly that documentation of a legal procedure out of state should be in the chart so that the patient can get the best possible care, whereas other doctors will say..., 'Why not avoid that language and just kind of be, you know, 'abstract' about it?'"

A recent *JAMA Health Forum* editorial by law professors Kayte Spector-Bagdady and Michelle Mello argues forcefully that medical providers should be aware that not only medical records but their own emails may be used by law enforcement officials prosecuting abortion. Doctors are not the only ones who are fearful. Barringer says that because of the current uncertainties, patients do not want details about past pregnancies documented or will not provide her with that information. Barringer adds that she sympathizes with their concerns but worries a lack of medical history "could interfere with providing the safest care possible in a future pregnancy."

Already, Barringer says, patients are concerned about sharing information on use of pills that induce an abortion—with or without a prescription—because of the Arkansas law that criminalizes harm to the fetus. New abortion restrictions that include language establishing "fetal rights" or "fetal personhood" will exacerbate existing disincentives to open communication. Michele Goodwin, a law professor at the University of California, Irvine, argues in her 2020 book *Policing the Womb* that there is increasing jeopardy for any pregnant person but particularly for those of color, who have historically been the target of prosecutorial overreach. With both genetic counselors and patients worried about what is safe to say, it will be harder than ever to establish the atmosphere of trust that is a bedrock of good medicine.

"Anecdotally," says a Texas genetic counselor, "I've already noticed some patients not wanting to fill out the intake form for pregnancies. And I've had people share things verbally they don't want to put in the paperwork." Not having the information impedes her ability to do her job. This might mean not knowing about an exposure to a drug, legal or illegal, that could affect fetal development. It might mean not learning about a previous pregnancy that ended in a miscarriage or abortion related to fetal health and therefore being unable to address the risk of the problem recurring.

Another genetic counselor mentions that in one recent case, a prenatal patient with abnormal ultrasound findings came to believe that the problems could have been caused by an abortion she had failed to disclose when she gave her medical history. Only after the patient felt comfortable enough to confide in her could the counselor correct the woman's misapprehensions and address her emotional needs. "She wanted to know if she caused this," the counselor says. "She had a lot of shame and guilt."

As attacks on access to abortion proliferate, genetic counselors worry that prenatal testing itself may become harder to access. Tests such as noninvasive prenatal testing (NIPT), which examines snippets of fetal DNA floating in the maternal bloodstream for missing or added DNA, are extremely popular with patients. But they can be seen as a stepping stone to abortion. In 2012 Republican presidential aspirant Rick Santorum was widely ignored when he said that health insurance companies should not be required to pay for amniocentesis because it was often used to "encourage abortion." Ten years later Santorum's position, while extreme, now must be taken seriously. "I can see that potentially being a problem," Barringer says, noting that Arkansas, like many other states, already prohibits insurance companies from offering policies that cover termination of pregnancy.

Restricting the use of expensive prenatal genetic testing to those who can pay for it out of pocket would effectively implement a lower standard of prenatal care for those who live in abortion-hostile states. Some would lose the opportunity to prevent the birth of a child with a genetic condition. Others–who would not have terminated–lose the chance to prepare for the birth of a child with special needs and to avoid a long and often arduous search for a diagnosis as evidence of a problem emerges postnatally.

Even for those who can afford it, prenatal genetic counseling may become increasingly hard to find. All four genetic counselors from Texas spoke movingly of an obligation to serve their patients, coupled with the strain of working in an environment in which they could not help them as they once did. In one email to *Scientific American*, a counselor from Dallas wrote that she worried for days about not providing information to a patient who asked for guidance on finding an abortion clinic out of state before deciding to share what she called "a minute amount of information." And then she worried for days afterward about "whether what I had said could be construed as aiding or abetting."

Genetic counseling is a limited resource. In a fast-growing field, demand continues to outstrip supply. Going forward, it may be hard to find candidates for positions whose "fringe benefits" include extra emotional burdens and potential legal liability. Barringer, contemplating laws that might restrict her ability to counsel patients as she has done for 25 years, is reluctantly considering what it would mean to turn away from a job she loves. "It's making me think, 'If that comes to fruition here, I don't know if, ethically, I'll be able to continue.' If I couldn't help my patients through some of the worst things that human beings can go through…, I honestly don't know what I would do."

About the Author

Laura Hercher is a genetic counselor and director of student research at the Joan H. Marks Graduate Program in Human Genetics at Sarah Lawrence College. She has written broadly on ethical, legal and social issues related to genetic medicine. Hercher is the host of The Beagle Has Landed, a podcast for the clinical genetics community and other sci-curious individuals.

Overturning *Roe v. Wade* Could Have Devastating Health and Financial Impacts, Landmark Study Showed

By Tanya Lewis

A leaked draft of a Supreme Court opinion suggests the nation's highest court is poised to overturn *Roe v. Wade*, the landmark ruling that guarantees the right to an abortion. The opinion was first reported by *Politico*. If it is officially issued later this year, nearly half of U.S. states will likely pass laws—or enforce existing ones—greatly restricting access to the procedure. One of the most comprehensive studies conducted to date shows that those who are denied an abortion—and thus forced to go through with an unwanted pregnancy—experience lasting impacts to their health, well-being, and finances.

A Supreme Court opinion along these lines has been expected, but the news nonetheless startled researchers who study reproductive rights. "The callousness of the decision is shocking," says Diana Greene Foster, a professor of obstetrics, gynecology, and reproductive sciences at the University of California, San Francisco.

Foster led the well-known Turnaway Study, a large and comprehensive investigation comparing women who received an abortion with women who were just past the legal gestational cutoff and were denied one. The study found that women denied the procedure were more likely to experience negative health impacts—including worse mental health—than women who received one. The former were also more likely to face worse financial outcomes, including poor credit, debt, and bankruptcy. (The study did not include pregnant people who did not identify as women.)

In May 2022, before the Supreme Court had issued its final opinion, *Scientific American* spoke to Foster about the Turnaway Study's findings and how a Supreme Court opinion overturning *Roe* would likely impact people seeking abortions in this country.

[An edited transcript of the interview follows.]

Q: What is your reaction to the leaked draft opinion that suggests *Roe* will be overturned?

A: This is the decision that I was anticipating because the abortion opinions of the justices are pretty well known. But the fact that it's leaked is shocking, unprecedented. And the callousness of the decision is kind of shocking, too—you know, the idea that the Constitution doesn't protect people's decision-making around something so fundamental as childbearing, when it has such huge impacts on their health and their ability to support themselves and their children.

And the idea that [*Roe v. Wade*] might have been wrongly decided—and how we would know that is that there is division within our country—that's not the principles of our Constitution. It's not about the division of our country; it's about the well-being of individuals. And so it's just the wrong motives.

Q: Can you describe the Turnaway Study and its main findings?

A: The Turnaway Study followed people who sought abortions—some who got their wanted abortion and some who were too far along and were denied. It looked at "What is the impact of having access to abortion on people's health and well-being?" And what we see is very large health burdens, greater health risks for people who carry pregnancies to term. That's consistent with the medical literature. We see greater complications from childbirth than from abortion, and in fact, two women in the study died after giving birth.

Q: In what other ways did being denied an abortion impact women and families?

A: We see economic hardship for people who had a child before they were ready, and we measure that through self-reported living in poverty—their income relative to household size—and we can also see it when we look at their credit reports. We can see that people who sought abortions had the same credit scores prior to the pregnancy, and after one group gave birth..., you can see in their credit records, you can see in their public financial records, that the group denied abortions experienced greater bankruptcies, evictions, and debt than other people who received their wanted abortion.

We actually see more economic hardship for children too. Often people say their reason for getting an abortion is to take care of the kids they already have. And [among those who are denied an abortion] we see those existing children are more likely to live in poverty, less likely to achieve developmental milestones than the children whose mothers were able to get an abortion.

Q: People often think that those seeking an abortion don't want to have kids at all. Is that true?

A: Many people who have abortions want to have children later, under better circumstances. And when they do—when they go and get an abortion and then go on and have a baby—we see those babies do better than children born because their mom was denied an abortion, in terms of the mom's emotional bond with the child, the kids' economic well-being, the chance that they live in a house with just enough money to pay for food and health.

Q: Are the people impacted by restrictive abortion laws disproportionately people of lower socioeconomic status?

A: Yes.

Q: Do you think the Supreme Court has ignored the science and the research on abortion?

A: I don't know that. I do know that when the case was heard, Supreme Court Justice John Roberts explicitly said, "[Put the] data aside." So that is not a good sign for him ruling on anything but ideological grounds–to not actually look at the evidence about how this affects families and decide just to do this on political or religious grounds.

Q: Have any amicus briefs in the current Supreme Court case, *Dobbs* v. *Jackson Women's Health Organization*, cited your research?

A: We have one amicus brief by social scientists. And there are two others that heavily cite my work–one by public health researchers and one by economists. And there's a whole amicus brief by the other side that is ... just an attempt to take down the Turnaway Study, but their criticisms are almost absurd.

They don't understand that, you know, people having unintended pregnancies, how common it is and the circumstances.

Q: Some studies looking at the effects of getting an abortion have compared people who had a child they wanted with those who sought an abortion. Is that a false comparison?

A: The people who wanted their child had better outcomes going in. It's not different people; it's people at different points–the same people under different circumstances. If you give someone a wanted abortion, they can later be the kind of person who can have a kid under circumstances that they do want. It's not that they're different people having kids; it's that people have to be able to have kids when they're ready.

There is a paper that actually compares outcomes for people who were forced to carry their pregnancy to term with the people who got an abortion and were able to have kids later on. Not all those subsequent pregnancies were planned in advance. Most of them weren't. But the person decided to carry that pregnancy to term, and the economic outcomes were better for that child, and the emotional outcomes were better as well.

Q: In your study, did the women who were denied legal abortions try to get them anyway?

A: In our study, they didn't, mostly. They either traveled vast distances and got an abortion somewhere else, or they had a baby. But the vast majority of them had the baby because there were very few places that would do abortions.

Q: Based on your research, what impact will this Supreme Court ruling have on pregnant people seeking abortions?

A: For people who are unable to get their abortion because the Supreme Court just lets states ban abortions, we're going to see worse physical health, greater economic hardship, lower achievement of aspirational plans, kids raised in more precarious economic circumstances, and people's lives upended.

About the Author

Tanya Lewis is a senior editor at Scientific American *who covers health and medicine.*

The Supreme Court's Abortion Ruling Upholds White Supremacy

By Biftu Mengesha

The recent Supreme Court decision in *Dobbs v. Jackson* erased the constitutional right to an abortion, immediately putting reproductive freedom in jeopardy for millions across the country. This unprecedented stripping of a legal and human right that people have relied on for 50 years intensified what was already a burgeoning reality on the ground for many. Now, as we approach midterm elections, with many local and state offices up for grabs, most abortions are banned in at least 14 states, and many more are likely to follow. This decision does not merely send the issue back to states; overturning *Roe* was a significant step in the antiabortion movement toward instituting a national ban on this procedure while instilling fetal personhood.

Unburdened access to safe abortion is an essential part of people retaining their ability to exercise their reproductive freedom and autonomy. These abortion restrictions violate autonomy in choosing if, when, and how someone engages in one of the most fundamental human experiences of reproduction. For centuries, the power to exercise reproductive freedom and to reproduce (or not) in a safe and dignified context has not been equitably distributed for marginalized communities and particularly for communities of color. Restrictions stemming from the *Dobbs* decision will undoubtedly bring further disparities of autonomy in communities of color, which will lead to a widening of the health and mortality disparities we currently see.

Black and Latinx communities proportionally have higher rates of abortion than white people, a consequence of structural and systemic barriers in health care and society more broadly. People of color are making decisions about the future of their families without equitable access to living wages, jobs, and reliable food and housing. Their families face the living legacy of redlining and housing segregation, along with inequities in education access, all of which limit their movement and upward mobility. Mass incarceration and our flawed justice system disrupt families, their participation in the workforce, and their contributions to society and voting. Widespread police violence destroys families, and Black parents fear police brutality before their children are even born.

Communities of color deal with barriers to health care and insurance and face racism and discrimination when they seek care, including narratives that blame people for social conditions that were created by the system. Worse yet, Black pregnant people face alarmingly high rates of pregnancy-related deaths in the hands of our health care system. Voter suppression and widespread attempts to disenfranchise communities prevent them from having a voice in transforming these structures that unjustly constrain them. This will beget further laws and restrictions that limit their rights and freedom—a modern manifestation of the separate-but-not-equal ideology of the Jim Crow era.

With these structures in mind—structures that primarily work to perpetuate barriers and poor outcomes for people of color—one thing about the *Dobbs* decision and the antiabortion movement becomes quite clear: this orchestrated attack on abortion rights sits within the grand plan that this country was built upon—the violent and oppressive maintenance of white supremacy.

As a Black cisgender woman and an abortion provider, I deeply fear what the unfolding of this very calculated move will do to my patients who look like me, to their families and to others from marginalized communities. As a physician who is committed to serving communities of color and helping them achieve the reproductive autonomy and well-being they deserve, I feel powerless seeing how the racist history of controlling our reproduction and freedom continues to be codified.

Throughout our country's history, people of color's fertility and reproduction have always been unjustly manipulated to benefit a white, misogynistic, xenophobic, homophobic, nationalist system. From forced reproduction that maintained slavery as an industry to forced sterilization and contraceptive abuses that limited mobility and growth and now to sweeping abortion restrictions that will disproportionately impact people of color, we continue to directly experience how white supremacy expertly sustains itself.

When people lose the right to exercise their bodily autonomy, we see significant effects on their own personal well-being and that of their communities. Denying someone the right to an abortion can lead to increased rates of infant and maternal mortality, poverty or lasting financial hardships, reduced ability to achieve aspirational goals, and worse mental health. For communities of color, this will have devastating impacts. Our country has pregnancy-related mortality rates far above those of other countries of similar economic development, and this is disproportionately shouldered by Black people who give birth. It is no coincidence that sweeping abortion restrictions are being imposed when our country is experiencing high rates of pregnancy-related mortality for people of color.

As people of color will now be forced to give birth, they will also be forced to experience an increased risk of dying from pregnancy. The lawmakers passing draconian abortion bans do nothing to avert this crisis by improving pregnancy or postpartum care and support for communities. With blood on the hands of those working to restrict abortion access, people of color will be further oppressed in our society, perpetuating the cycle of unjust and deadly social conditions.

This is not to say that if these social conditions didn't exist, people wouldn't seek abortion. Abortion is normal and necessary and should always be an unburdened option for people to choose for themselves. Rather it's reckoning with the reality that reproductive decisions do not occur in isolation of the structural injustices that significantly influence people's health and livelihood. They are making these decisions while gripped by the stranglehold of white supremacy. Burdening communities of color with being unable to vote freely, move freely, express their gender and sexuality freely, work and thrive and keep their families safe–and now with not being able to make their reproductive decisions freely–reinforces these intentional injustices.

Marginalized communities, and particularly communities of color, have proved time and again that they will overcome and achieve their liberation in all ways necessary, even in the face of deadly injustices. They are wholly capable of realizing their power to create change, as they have for centuries. Marginalized communities have led the way in the most preeminent social movements in this country and will continue to do so with courage and conviction.

A real commitment to fighting these injustices and saving lives means that white people in particular must shift power and resources to those communities and follow their leadership toward achieving self-determination and liberation. We need to move people of color into positions of power and protect their constitutional right to exercise their voices so they can make necessary changes.

We need to provide avenues for communities of color to thrive and have the same freedoms without burden or harm as white people have had for centuries. In order to realize reproductive justice and allow people to live their life with dignity and safety, we need to work to protect those who are directly in harm's way from this restrictive landscape of abortion access.

This is an opinion and analysis article, and the views expressed by the author or authors are not necessarily those of Scientific American.

About the Author

Biftu Mengesha (she/her) is an obstetrician-gynecologist and complex family planning subspecialist at the University of California, San Francisco, where she does abortion education, advocacy and research. She is associate fellowship program director of the Complex Family Planning fellowship, associate ob-gyn residency program director and director of Innovating Education in Reproductive Health, which is a freely available online resource for sexual and reproductive health curricula, particularly for abortion and contraception.

What the Supreme Court Should Know about Abortion Care

By Cara C. Heuser

Abortion makes many people uncomfortable. I get it. When I was an ob-gyn resident, I recall telling my supervising physician that I would learn the skills to perform an abortion, but probably wouldn't provide them after I graduated because doing so made me "a little uncomfortable."

My supervising physician asked me in response, "Do you think women have a right to this procedure?" I thought, "Well ... yeah, of course."

With the leaked decision in *Dobbs v. Jackson Women's Health Organization*, the Supreme Court has indicated its willingness to place a heavy brick on the scale of the statue of Lady Justice, who graces the Supreme Court building. The goal of law, as with medicine, should always be to find the balance between benefit and harm. The justices have landed squarely on the side of harm.

Balancing the scales will require a concerted and sustained effort. Most Americans fall in the "muddy middle" of the abortion debate and may be reluctant to wade into the fraught waters. Again, this hesitancy is understandable. Abortion is an uncomfortable topic for many people. However, people who have been passive on this issue can no longer be so. If this is you, it's not too late. Let your lawmakers know where you stand on this issue. Have the difficult conversations with your family and friends about why you support bodily autonomy. Donate to organizations doing this work.

Here's why: when I was a young doctor unsure of my willingness to provide abortions, my supervisor and I talked about how I perhaps have an ethical and moral obligation to do my part in assuring that the procedure is available. Because it's not about me, or my comfort, or you, or anyone, except the person seeking care. So, almost 20 years later, in addition to prenatal care and deliveries of complex pregnancies, I now also provide abortions and teach new doctors how to do them.

I do this because people have a right to this procedure but also because this medical adage resonates with me: "May I never see in the patient anything but a fellow creature in pain." This is not to imply that every abortion decision must be a painful one (although some are), but rather a reminder to put patient needs first.

I have this somewhat starry-eyed idea that if anti-abortion crusaders could spend a few days in my office, they would start to get it. While that daydream may seem naive, the fact is that many patients who identify as "pro-life" have sat in my office after unexpected news about their pregnancy and expressed to me that they have a new understanding of these nuanced issues. They can now see the harm in the laws they formerly supported.

I have written before about how providing medical care that both honors birth and upholds a person's right not to carry a pregnancy is not a contradiction. The well-accepted medical ethical principles of beneficence, nonmaleficence, justice, and autonomy compel me to provide full-spectrum reproductive care. If the leaked opinion on *Dobbs* stands, it will prevent me from providing the full suite of obstetrical care and upend 50 years of precedent that preserves the right to end a pregnancy. The case challenges the 2018 Mississippi Gestational Age Act, which prohibits abortions after 15 weeks with few exceptions. Petitioners also asked the court to overturn precedent establishing a constitutional right to previability abortions, the end results of *Roe v. Wade* and *Planned Parenthood of Southeastern Pennsylvania v. Casey*. States will now be the main legislators of abortion and can force people to give birth against their will. More than 20 states already have abortion bans designed to quickly take effect if the court rules these laws constitutional, with the most restrictive banning abortion almost completely.

This is terrible news for anyone who values bodily autonomy, separation of church and state, and opposes government interference into science and medicine. While we cannot eliminate individual values and morality from this debate, if we accept the premise that medicine is an applied science, it is worth examining the science behind why abortion restrictions are harmful.

Multiple studies have confirmed that abortion restrictions do more harm than good, that abortion is safe, and that the oft-cited concern that having an abortion is detrimental to mental health is not true. The most well-known of these studies is the decade-long Turnaway Study, the main finding of which is that receiving an abortion does not harm health and well-being, but in fact, being denied an abortion results in worse financial, health, and family outcomes.

Most people don't realize that carrying a pregnancy to term is 14 times more dangerous than an early legal abortion. While we should work to reduce the maternal mortality rate, especially among women of color, the fact is that being pregnant (or being forced to seek an unsafe or illegal abortion) is always going to be riskier than a safely performed abortion.

The harm of abortion restrictions is why mainstream medical societies oppose them. Examples include the American College of Obstetrics and Gynecology, the Society for Maternal Fetal Medicine, the American Academy of Pediatrics, the American Psychiatric Association, and the American Academy of Family Physicians. The American Medical Association has voiced opposition to the most restrictive laws. These are not radical fringe organizations, but groups made up of the physicians living in your community and caring for you every day.

Technology has continued to advance since the original abortion decisions in 1973 and 1992. New techniques in medical and surgical abortions continue to reduce the already low complication rate. Home pregnancy tests have become increasingly sensitive, allowing people to recognize a pregnancy without a physician visit. Diagnostic techniques in ultrasound and genetics have expanded exponentially, allowing detection of complications that would not have been known until after birth in 1973.

As we face an onslaught of anti-abortion state legislation, we should be prepared with an idea of how to best balance the scales to offer the greatest benefit for the least harm. It is my opinion, as a physician who has dedicated her career to helping pregnant individuals and babies have the best outcomes, that the best way to do this is to remove all restrictions on abortions. This is not an extreme position.

While some people might conclude it is appropriate to limit abortion after a certain point in pregnancy and to limit the reasons for terminating a pregnancy, pregnancy is one of the most complex biological processes—and thus the ways in which it can go awry are myriad and complex. Decisions that a person makes with their doctor require a nuanced consideration of individual values and circumstances, rather than a generalized approach that can be legislated; this was part of the argument in *Roe v. Wade*.

Even the concept of "viability," upon which SCOTUS based previous decisions, is nebulous and dynamic as a consequence of the evolving nature of medicine. The likelihood that any fetus will survive outside the uterus as a neonate is an estimate based on many factors. Furthermore, as technology advances, prognoses will change. Viability is a poor legal standard. If Justice Samuel Alito did anything right in the leaked opinion, it was to abandon viability as a benchmark.

Dogmatic laws presume a certainty that rarely exists in the realities of clinical medicine. They fail to account for the range of prognoses that characterize many conditions, as well as how the complexities of psychosocial circumstances, mental health, and disparities in access to care affect a person's health outcomes. Lawmakers cannot possibly legislate every circumstance or exception that must exist to prevent sometimes significant harm and/or suffering. Biology constantly surprises us.

After removing abortion restrictions, we should next dismantle other barriers to care. As others have described, it is not just laws that limit choice. It doesn't help that abortion is legal if you can't afford it, can't get time off, don't have transportation, or have myriad other systemic constraints. The Hyde Amendment, which prohibits federally funded insurances like Medicaid from covering abortions, needs to sink without bubbles. The FDA's unnecessary restrictions on mifepristone, a common and safe abortifacient, also have got to go. We should support and promote the many excellent organizations helping people access care and dismantle barriers. Finally, as reproductive choice is about choice, we need systems in place to support individuals who choose to stay pregnant and/or parent. None of the above require a Supreme Court decision. Many could, and should, be legislated by Congress or implemented by executive order.

In addition to her scale, Lady Justice holds a double-edged sword. She wears a blindfold. It appears our highest court will not wield this sword responsibly with regards to abortion, and the blindfolds some of the justices wear with regard to body autonomy need to come off. The work of preserving abortion rights belongs to everyone—not just people who can become pregnant. My patients deserve to make decisions about their bodies without ideological interference. So do you.

This is an opinion and analysis article, and the views expressed by the author or authors are not necessarily those of Scientific American.

About the Author

Cara C. Heuser is a maternal-fetal medicine physician. She provides full-spectrum reproductive care, including prenatal care for high-risk pregnancies and abortion care, in Salt Lake City.

Section 7: Points of View

Abortion Bans Based on So-Called "Science" Are Fraudulent

By Nicole M. Baran, Gretchen Goldman, and Jane Zelikova

We are scientists, and we believe that evidence, not ideology, should inform health-care decisions. The wave of anti-abortion laws across the U.S. is the latest in a long string of attempts to falsely use the language and authority of science to justify denying people their basic human rights and inflict lasting harm. Although abortion is still legal in every state, recent legislation in Alabama, Georgia, Kentucky, Louisiana, Mississippi, Missouri, and Ohio threatens the future of abortion rights in the country. Scientists should, first and foremost, value evidence, and the evidence is clear: abortion bans cause harm. They make abortions less safe and especially harm historically marginalized communities.

As scientists, we are uniquely positioned to use our privilege and position in society to speak against the new abortion bans and other public policies that threaten the reproductive freedom of our nation's people. We have the knowledge to communicate the science of reproductive health care, demonstrate the harm restrictive laws will cause, and hold decision makers to account.

The public officials behind these latest abortion bans exhibit breathtaking ignorance of the science of their own proposals. When asked when a woman would still be able to obtain an abortion under his near-total ban, Alabama State Senator Clyde Chambliss uttered "I'm at the limits of my medical knowledge, but until those chromosomes you were talking about combine—from male and female—that's my understanding." The lawmaker is clearly confused about the fundamentals of reproductive science, but that hasn't stopped him from authoring the most restrictive abortion law in the country—one that threatens the health of his constituents.

So-called heartbeat bills, which ban abortion as early as after six weeks of pregnancy, are not based on science. In fact, no heart yet exists in an embryo at six weeks. Yet six states and counting enacted such bills in 2019, in addition to Alabama's near-total ban. Equally unscientific "abortion reversal" laws are also gaining traction. These laws, now on the books in eight states, require doctors to tell patients receiving a medication abortion, a safe and effective way to end an early pregnancy, that it can be reversed halfway through to save their pregnancy.

Not only is this law bad science, it is actively dangerous. The idea of abortion reversal is based on a single study of six participants that was (poorly) conducted without an ethics review board. The so-called abortion reversal procedure is experimental and has neither been clinically tested nor approved by the Food and Drug Administration. Both heartbeat bills and abortion reversal laws have been opposed by leading medical groups, including the American Medical Association and the American College of Obstetricians and Gynecologists.

Our Complacency Is Complicity

As scientists, it is our job to assess the evidence, and what we know from many countries, including the U.S., is that that restrictions to reproductive health do not stop abortions but make them less safe. In addition, attempts to limit access to legal and safe abortion violate basic human rights and increase unsafe abortions. These abortion bans will cost lives—period. Existing restrictions in more than half of U.S. states already limit access to timely and affordable abortions, and these new laws would take such constraints to new heights. For example, miscarriages may be "investigated" and prosecuted under the recent law passed in Georgia. Because one in four pregnancies end in miscarriage, such scrutiny would undoubtedly target and further traumatize people already dealing with the loss of a pregnancy.

The elected officials passing these laws are not concerned with medical expertise or scientific evidence. They actively misrepresent the work of scientists, using rhetoric to deceive the public and stoke emotional outrage. These abortion bans are ideological and cynical, they are appallingly unscientific, and they are dangerous. We need leaders who will use science to create a safer world for all, and we, as scientists and citizens, need to hold them accountable when they don't. It is time for scientists to show up and use our voices, money, and positions of privilege to push back on these oppressive and harmful abortion bans.

For too long, scientists have been afraid to wade into controversies because we were taught to believe that being outspoken would chip away at our perceived public credibility. But our persistent silence has made us complicit. Anti-choice groups continue to invoke science in support of their cause. Case in point: this year the March for Life, a protest against the practice and legality of abortion, falsely claimed that science is on the side of the anti-choice movement.

In the past, as we stood on the sidelines, science was misrepresented and weaponized to harm people. We must not only face the historical legacy of that harm but also realize that the same tactics are being used today to perpetuate oppression. And we have to vow to break our silence. The time is now. We must stand in solidarity with health-care workers, activists, organizers, and all who fight for reproductive justice and human rights—today and every day.

Reckoning with Science's History of Harm

Unfortunately, these latest laws build upon a long history of racist and misogynistic policies that invoke science to justify the control of people's bodies and to specifically target women and members of marginalized communities. The "science" of eugenics was used to justify sterilizing women of color and disabled people for decades. The long-disproven practice of conversion therapy is still used today in an attempt to change people's sexual orientation. Even the scientific understanding of women's biological roles as mothers and nurturers continues to be twisted to defend the patriarchy, leading some to continue to argue that the subordination and domesticity of women is somehow the "natural" moral order of the world.

It is worth remembering that historically marginalized people have long suffered directly at the hands of science. The inventor of the vaginal speculum performed horrific experiments on enslaved women. A government experiment spanning decades allowed hundreds of rural African American men with syphilis to go untreated. And the HeLa cells that revolutionized modern medicine were taken from a poor, African American woman as she was dying of cervical cancer without her consent or any kind of compensation for her or her descendants.

It is no surprise that the modern anti-abortion agenda itself is grounded in racism and shoddy science. The long history of using science to demonize Black women and justify laws that exert control over their bodies equates to institutionally sanctioned violence. Although scientific research has provided the world with much good, it has also caused harm to countless individuals, especially people of color and sexual and gender minorities. This is a truth we must confront and a history we must not repeat.

Marginalized People Will Be Disproportionately Affected by Restrictions to Reproductive Health Care

The negative effects of restricting access to safe and affordable reproductive health services will not be evenly felt. The efforts to ban access to abortion affect all people who can get pregnant, but they create additional risks for low-income women, women of color, trans men, and genderqueer people, as well as victims of intimate-partner violence or sexual abuse, who are already navigating a health-care system stacked against them. Long-established restrictive laws, such as waiting periods, parental-consent requirements, state-mandated counseling, and conditions for hospital admitting privileges, have imposed disproportionate barriers to reproductive freedom for these groups for decades.

Marginalized people who want to end their pregnancy may feel unsafe disclosing this information or even seeking the help they need because of the stigma or the risk of violence. Women of color already face appalling maternal mortality and infant death rates. By minimizing access to safe abortions, these women and their children will be subjected to additional risks of death and injury.

None of the recent laws include provisions for emotional, community, or financial support for parents and babies. Forcing people to carry unwanted pregnancies to term, especially without addressing the multifaceted challenges associated with bringing a baby into the world, will only worsen the mental and physical health disparities and socioeconomic challenges for groups already disproportionately affected by these struggles.

Access to reproductive health care is not a women's issue–it is a human rights issue. Everyone benefits when people have access to health services and when they have autonomy to start their families on their own personal timelines.

Now Is the Time to Act

What can and should scientists do? Follow the lead of groups who have been on the front lines of these issues. Women of color have been leading the movement against this latest onslaught of policies that limit access to safe reproductive health care, as well as the reproductive restrictions that came before. Ongoing organizing and legal action by these groups, especially in the American South, have helped ensure greater access to reproductive care for those living in states with barriers to abortion access. Local groups, such as SisterSong, SPARK Reproductive Justice NOW, Access Reproductive Care–Southeast, and Feminist Women's Health Center, and national groups, including the American Civil Liberties Union, Planned Parenthood, and NARAL Pro-Choice America, need support to continue their work in the face of new bans. We should listen to these organizers and follow their example.

You should donate money if you can, but you can also help in many other ways. You can participate in local direct actions, including marches, educational events, and organizing meetings. You can also volunteer to help transport or house women who need to travel long distances for an abortion or become an abortion clinic escort or abortion doula. You can even act as a medical model and help educate health-care professionals on how to provide comfortable, affirming and culturally competent reproductive care for all people.

And men, your efforts are especially welcome: here are some tips. We need to know that we are not alone in this fight.

Supporting on-the-ground initiatives is critical, but we must also look within our own research programs and consider the potential negative impact of our work and the ways it may affect vulnerable people. If you are involved in any human studies, think carefully about their design to ensure that harms to vulnerable communities are minimized and work to make sure that the benefits of your research are also just and equitable. If you are in a position of gatekeeper, prioritize the funding, publication, and dissemination of research that is guided by justice and equity. As an instructor in the sciences, ensure that you are providing your students with the tools to understand and evaluate scientific information but also respect and acknowledge other ways of knowing.

Use your position of authority to advocate for evidence-based sex education in your local schools and science-based decision-making from your local public officials. Do not be afraid to use your voice and your power.

You can educate yourself and others on the reproductive justice movement here, here and here.

And if you or someone you know are currently struggling to access abortion care anywhere in the U.S., you can find more information here.

The views expressed are those of the author(s) and are not necessarily those of Scientific American.

About the Authors

Nicole M. Baran is a postdoctoral fellow at Georgia Institute of Technology and a visiting scholar at Emory University. She is a behavioral neuroscientist who studies the evolution of social behavior in both birds and fish, including pair bonding, parental behaviors, mating strategies, aggression, and vocal learning. She is the executive coordinator of the 500 Women Scientists Atlanta pod.

Gretchen Goldman is the research director for the Center for Science and Democracy at the Union of Concerned Scientists and air pollution exposure scientist. She holds a Ph.D. and M.S. in environmental engineering from the Georgia Institute of Technology, and a B.S. in atmospheric science from Cornell University.

Jane Zelikova is an ecologist interested in the impacts of environmental change on natural and managed ecosystems. Her interests are broad and include tropical biogeochemistry, as well as the effects of climate change on organisms big and small. She combines a strong emphasis on research with an interest in science communication and outreach, thinking about ways to expand the role of science in tackling global issues. She is the co-founder of 500 Women Scientists.

How Abortion Misinformation and Disinformation Spread Online

By Jenna Sherman

The Supreme Court's decision to curtail abortion rights has come to fruition. One of the outcomes that will be less discussed is how more people in states with heavy restrictions will turn to search engines and social media to figure out how now to manage their reproductive decisions, and will find themselves reading questionable information. The information they'll find could be questionable; the number of false and misleading statements online about abortion has grown since the draft opinion on *Dobbs v. Jackson Women's Health Organization* was leaked in May, and with the decision now handed down, it will undoubtedly increase.

Perhaps no medical procedure is subject to more misinformation than abortion, and social media and search engine companies have been too stagnant in their efforts to stop the spread. Access to safe abortion is reaching a point of no return, and we no longer have time for this level of inaction on abortion mis- and disinformation. Internet companies need to stop accepting advertising money from groups that lie about abortion, and they need to do a better job of removing posts with false information. Such information isn't just confusing or a nuisance. Misinformation has been shown to influence people's decisions—and in this case the decisions being influenced are about reproductive health, with the potential to lead to tangible consequences such as shame around abortion decision-making and complicated, unsafe abortion.

First, some definitions: abortion *misinformation* is the unintentional spread of false or misleading information about the physical and psychological risks or consequences of getting an abortion. Abortion *disinformation* is similar but is intentionally spread to promote an antiabortion agenda. To be clear, the two cannot be fully dichotomized, as disinformation often (intentionally) begets misinformation when someone naively spreads falsehoods created by someone with disingenuous aims.

I am very familiar with disinformation and political agendas. Growing up in Texas suburbs and rural Alabama, I regularly heard the message in school, from doctors, and from community members that abortion was harmful and shameful. Now that I study health misinformation, focusing on online information about reproductive health, it's clear to me that these admonishments were rife with disinformation and pushed by a religious and political agenda–not a public health one. But far too many people aren't able to make these distinctions online.

I need only to turn to my phone to find the same narratives, posted by people such as nefarious antiabortion actors to concerned, religious mothers. If I search for abortion information on social media or a search engine, I quickly come into contact with false claims like "abortion is never medically necessary" and "women are at risk of injury, infertility, and possible death from the chemical abortion pill"

Research has made clear that much of the content people find online about abortion is not reliable, and commonly includes disinformation that seeks to misinform and thwart abortion access. Much like the messages I received growing up in the Deep South, these messages carry religious and political undertones that are difficult to distinguish from objective, evidence-based information. This is on purpose. Antichoice websites regularly publish intentionally misleading or false information about abortion in a manner that presents as objective in an effort to mask the fact that it's antiscience. And depending on several factors, search engines sometimes push these sites to the top of result pages over more evidence-based ones.

This is the bleak future for science-based reproductive health decisions; the highest volume of online searches about abortion are in the states with the most restricted access. Even a change in local policies on abortion in the U.S. is associated with more attempts to find abortion information online.

Despite the federal change to health-care rights, abortion shame and stigma and a lack of access to quality health information or care from professionals are already reasons why anyone might seek information online. Women of color and people with low incomes disproportionately experience reproductive injustice, and as a result their need for accurate abortion information is especially critical.

And should you think that social media platforms are passive bystanders in this problem, just conduits for information, think again. They regularly profit from it.

The Center for Countering Digital Hate reports that from January 2020 to September 2021, Facebook alone accepted between $115,400 and $140,667 for 92 ads promoting "abortion pill reversal"–the use of progesterone to reverse a medication abortion in its early stages. This procedure is unproven and unethical, and was stopped in clinical trials because it caused dangerous hemorrhaging. The center's report also found that a whopping 83 percent of searches for abortion carried an ad for "abortion reversal," meaning that the vast majority of Google searches on abortion when the study was conducted surfaced disinformation that was disguised as neutral and helpful. And while Google and Facebook have both worked to clamp down on the issue of false and misleading ads about abortion, they have not done enough.

And of course, the problem is not just ads. Social media posts and search engine results also yield misleading information about abortion. One 2021 study found that, of the five top results for "abortion pill" on Google, only one contained information that was scientifically accurate and moderately accessible–meaning written at a lower grade level in plain language that's easy for a reader to digest. Three were from overtly antiabortion groups, and they spread disinformation and misinformation about abortion pills.

Another study found that over half of the web pages on abortion surfaced by Google contained misinformation that could hinder a person's decision to have one by pushing claims that abortion is unsafe and referring them to covertly antiabortion "health" centers using scare tactics.

As of this writing, a simple Google search of "abortion pill reversal" surfaced a website endorsing the safety and efficacy of abortion pill reversal as the first result, listed above a webpage from the American College of Obstetricians and Gynecologists stating that this reversal process is not supported by science.

These search results primarily stem from crisis pregnancy centers, which are legal but unethical. Abortion misinformation and disinformation aren't just inconvenient and misleading; they can affect a person's ability to make informed health decisions and increase feelings of shame, confusion, and stigma. Given that conducting causal research on misinformation and its effects is challenging, there are likely further, unknown health consequences.

These mis- and disinformation narratives online are mirrored in antichoice legislation. One 2016 analysis by the National Partnership for Women and Families found that 70 percent of state-level abortion restrictions introduced in 2016 were based on antiabortion lies.

This also applies to the *Dobbs* opinion. In the opinion, the justices cite the 2007 case *Gonzales v. Carhart*, which upheld the Partial-Birth Abortion Ban Act and signaled a shift in the court toward restricting abortion. They say that most abortions after 15 weeks "for non therapeutic or elective reasons [are] a barbaric practice, dangerous for the maternal patient, and demeaning to the medical profession." The draft ruling also insinuates that fetuses feel pain before the third trimester and that restricting abortion preserves the "protection of maternal health" as well as "the prevention of discrimination on the basis of race, sex, or disability."

Each of these statements is medically inaccurate. For instance, basing a decision off of abortions post-15 weeks is illogical and misleading considering that the vast majority of abortions (about 93% as of 2019 in the U.S.) are performed at or before 13 weeks. These misleading statements also represent the same narratives circulating on social media and stemming from antiabortion groups, such as crisis pregnancy centers and the group Live Action, which regularly makes claims online that abortion is unsafe.

This opinion signals the Supreme Court's continued shift from decisions based on science and evidence to ones based on political and religious ideology, and reflects the increasingly blurred line between antiscience narratives that primarily spread online and real-world antiscience policy and legislation. The two directly and inextricably influence one another.

The rise of mis- and disinformation about abortion demonstrate how political and religious ideologues are able to successfully game an internet system that has inadequate checks and balances, and how those narratives can go on to become "truths" that are legally codified. Social media companies are more than complicit actors–they are enablers. Now is the time to act. The people who use these platforms have a right to honest, factual information in making enormous life decisions such as whether or not to continue a pregnancy. The question at stake is not just what actions are we willing to take to protect abortion access, but how far are we willing to let technology influence not only our opinions, but our health and livelihoods?

This is an opinion and analysis article, and the views expressed by the author or authors are not necessarily those of Scientific American.

About the Author

Jenna Sherman is a program manager at Meedan's Digital Health Lab where she works on the intersection of technology and reproductive health equity. She holds an M.P.H. from the Harvard T.H. Chan School of Public Health.

Abortion Doesn't Have to Be an Either-Or Conversation

By Amy Alspaugh, Linda S. Franck, Renée Mehra, Daniel Suárez-Baquero, Nikki Lanshaw, Toni Bond, and Monica R. McLemore

The language we use to talk about a pregnant person's right to decide whether to continue a pregnancy is full of false binaries: pro-choice versus pro-life, bodily autonomy versus fetal personhood, moral versus immoral. These dualities unnecessarily divide us and prevent deeper conversations about the unique status of pregnancy within our society.

An either-or mentality creates a situation of separate but unequal laws for pregnant people that violate both the human right to bodily autonomy and the guarantee of equal protection under the law.

We, as nurses, midwives, and health researchers, know that using a both-and mentality instead of an either-or mentality makes space for multiple truths and nondichotomist positions concerning the decision to continue or terminate a pregnancy. A both-and approach is a hallmark of Black feminism and one that assumes multiple outcomes, multiple discussions, or multiple futures as we work together to address the urgent reproductive health crisis in our country.

The primary issue in the *Dobbs v. Jackson Women's Health* Supreme Court case is whether or not Mississippi's 15-week, previability abortion ban is constitutional. When *Roe v. Wade* was argued, however, the word "viability" was never uttered. Court documents show how a Supreme Court clerk suggested that viability be settled upon as a *legal* compromise. That compromise attempted to mark to a point in time at which, in the prescient words of Justice Thurgood Marshall, "the State's interest in preserving the potential life of the unborn child overrides any individual interests of the woman."

The binary status of viability and nonviability means that the rights of pregnant people are time-sensitive. As we've learned from the experiences of countless marginalized groups, rights that do not apply to all individuals at all times are not rights, but conditional benefits that are inequitably distributed. The emphasis in the abortion debate on viability distracts us from the human rights argument that asserts that bodily autonomy, including the decision to continue or terminate a pregnancy, rests squarely with the pregnant person *at all times and in all circumstances.*

The whipping of Black enslaved people who were pregnant is a noted instance of the false dichotomy of promoting survival of the fetus at the expense of the pregnant person's humanity and autonomy. To protect these fetuses, the enslaved people's stomachs lay in holes dug into the ground while the rest of their bodies were exposed for punishment. Repeatedly, lawmakers and law enforcers have justified the primacy of fetal rights to restrict bodily autonomy and enforce separate, distinct laws over the bodies and decisions of pregnant people—especially pregnant people of color.

The push for fetal personhood developed alongside, and is in many ways tied to, scientific advances in perinatal-neonatal medicine that enabled the fetus to survive (with extensive technological life support) outside the uterus at earlier and earlier gestations. In this way the fetus and pregnant person became separate entities, and separate patients in a health-care setting.

Abortion binaries exist not only in legal settings, but in social discourse. For decades, a majority of adults in the United States has agreed that abortion should be legal in all or most cases. However, heterogeneity in views on abortion, particularly across religious affiliations and political ideologies, provide evidence of more nuanced beliefs within groups. Therefore, representations of individuals as either "pro-life" or "pro-choice" do little to identify the granular detail behind an individual's attitudes, beliefs, and behavior.

These binary beliefs provide little context around people's life circumstances and the communities in which they belong. Our recent research identified obstetric, women's health, and neonatal nurses' attitudes around abortion. We found that on a five-point scale (i.e., strongly or moderately proabortion, or strongly or moderately antiabortion, or unsure) that used 14 questions to measure abortion attitudes, one-third of the participants ended up in the unsure category. They were neither proabortion or antiabortion. This category also included the largest percentage of those who identified as Christian.

Among nurses who took the survey and reported having had an abortion, nearly one-quarter were in the unsure category and 10 percent vocalized antiabortion attitudes, indicating that people's attitudes about abortion are not necessarily indicative of their behavior. This may be evidence of internalized abortion stigma. A lack of concordance between attitudes and actions is neither new nor problematic, but instead points to the importance of meeting people where they are, and respecting their expertise and ability to know exactly what is best of them and their families.

Moving away from binaries and polarities allows us to instead focus on language that helps create physical and social environments that ensure equitable reproductive health for all, a healthy pregnancy for all who choose parenthood, and a safe childhood for all. Research suggests that many people who had an abortion wanted to continue the pregnancy and parent the child but made the choice to have an abortion because they felt they could not adequately or ethically raise a child. They often cited circumstances specific to a lack of resources, whether human, money, space, or time.

Often, these circumstances could have been ameliorated by enhanced social services, legal protections for pregnant people, paid parental leave, and universal childcare, but instead pit the needs of the fetus against the needs of the parent. Policies that are centered in reproductive justice can address the biggest threats to life and livelihood; namely poverty, health-care barriers, racism, and environmental hazards. Meeting these needs could reduce the need for abortion.

Regardless of the decision of the Supreme Court, we as healthcare providers and researchers must do a better job allowing for complexity. What do pregnant people want and need? Are we implementing policies that provide financial security, high-quality health care, and the social support necessary for those that desire to grow their family while simultaneously ensuring safe, respectful and stigma-free abortion services are readily accessible?

With the future of safe and legal abortion in the hands of the Supreme Court, we affirm that bodily autonomy as manifested in abortion is a human right, and at the same time, we must improve health care and social services for all people who choose parenthood, especially those historically marginalized.

About the Authors

Amy Alspaugh is a certified nurse-midwife in Knoxville, TN, and has a Ph.D. in Nursing. She currently works as an assistant professor at the University of Tennessee College of Nursing, where she researches women's reproductive health.

Linda S. Franck holds the Jack and Elaine Koehn Endowed Chair in Pediatric Nursing at the University of California, San Francisco, School of Nursing and co-directs the ACTIONS fellowship program. She leads family and community partnered research in maternal, newborn, child and adolescent healthcare.

Renée Mehra, Ph.D., an ACTIONS postdoctoral scholar at University of California, San Francisco, explores the social and structural factors that influence racial and ethnic inequities in maternal and infant health. She uses mixed-method research to examine policies, programs, and health-care delivery models that may reduce these inequities.

Daniel Felipe Martín Suárez-Baquero is a postdoctoral fellow in the ACTIONS program at the University of California, San Francisco. He received his Ph.D. in Nursing from the University of Texas at Austin and his BSN and MSN in Maternal/Perinatal Nursing Care from the Universidad Nacional de Colombia. His research and practice concern Latina/e's reproductive health experiences, community/cultural memory of ethnic minoritized women, and nursing theory.

Nikki Lanshaw, MPH, is the Project Director of the Abortion Care Training Incubator for Outstanding Nurse Scholars (ACTIONS) program at University of California, San Francisco. Her work focuses on policy interventions to improve access to reproductive health care and health insurance coverage.

Toni Bond, Ph.D., is a womanist scholar and ethicist. Her research focuses on the lives of Black women and the intersectionality between religion and reproductive justice, womanist theology, and womanist ethics. She currently works as an ACTIONS postdoctoral fellow at the University of California, San Francisco, School of Nursing.

Monica R. McLemore is an associate professor in the Family Health Care Nursing Department and a clinician-scientist at Advancing New Standards in Reproductive Health at the University of California, San Francisco.

Primary Care Providers Can Help Safeguard Abortion

By Diana Carvajal, Casandra Cashman, and Ian Lague

The Supreme Court has overturned constitutional protections for abortion, and several states have now immediately outlawed essential care that is used by roughly one in four Americans who can become pregnant. As many people in the health professions have said, these prohibitions will undermine bodily autonomy, criminalize a wide range of pregnancy outcomes, and limit the personal and professional lives of millions of Americans. They will also undoubtedly increase pregnancy-related morbidity and mortality.

As educators and physicians who provide abortions, we believe that this vital health service must not be limited to abortion clinics and ob-gyn practices. They are already overburdened in our shifting legal landscape. America urgently needs to expand and diversify its abortion care workforce, and primary care providers are key to that expansion. Family physicians, internists, pediatricians, nurse practitioners, and certified midwives care for people who are pregnant. They can, and do, safely and effectively provide both medication and procedural abortions in their offices, but only 3 percent of family physicians provide abortion care.

As a matter of health equity, many more primary care clinicians should step up to provide the abortion services that fall well within their scope of practice. Many people prefer to access abortion and other sexual and reproductive health services from their primary care physicians, who are usually their first and main source of health care. In addition, providing abortions within primary care reduces stigma and enhances continuity with other health care services. It also increases access to abortion.

Access is a key issue here. The right to abortion has been eroded for decades by restrictive state laws, federal funding bans, conservative courts, and structural inequities rooted in racism, misogyny, and xenophobia. Low-income, rural, Black, indigenous, and immigrant communities are and will be even more disproportionately harmed by forced birth and the criminalization of miscarriage and self-managed abortion. Overzealous prosecutors are already charging people who abort (or even miscarry) with crimes.

While telehealth and self-managed medication abortion may reduce some of the harm caused by abortion bans, many pregnant people won't be able to access these services, whether because lacking in funds, internet access, or a secure mailing address. In addition, 19 states currently prohibit telemedicine abortion provision, and some patients will be medically ineligible for remote services. This will worsen reproductive injustice and inequity, continuing to sow mistrust among marginalized people.

In states where abortion ends up completely banned, primary care practices will face many of the same legal and financial risks as dedicated abortion facilities. Yet primary care clinicians can play a pivotal role in helping to meet the surge in demand that is already overwhelming abortion clinics in sanctuary and border states. Rural and exurban areas of states already bear the brunt of the abortion provider shortage, something that is likely to increase sharply if *Roe* is overturned. These are often regions where primary care clinicians are the sole providers of health care, including sexual and reproductive health. Patients in rural areas are often already at a disadvantage when trying to access health care, including abortion, as most abortion providers are concentrated in larger cities, which requires patients to manage transportation, lodging, childcare, and lost wages. Primary care abortion providers could substantially reduce these burdens, because many of these clinicians will be situated much closer to restricted states.

Expanding the primary care abortion workforce is not without challenges. Abortion providers tend to be clustered around academic medical centers that are often located in urban areas and states with fewer abortion restrictions. The abortion care workforce, like the general medical workforce, has a severe lack of racial/ethnic diversity. Such diversity is critical for building trust, improved health outcomes and mitigation of health disparities, problems that will be aggravated by new restrictions on abortion and sexual and reproductive healthcare.

However, there is good evidence that change is possible, particularly within family medicine. When family medicine residents train at programs that include abortion education as part of routine instruction, their rate of providing abortions increases dramatically after graduation, to 29 percent. And, while the underrepresentation of Black, indigenous, and Latinx clinicians is rooted in the deeply racist evolution of U.S. medical professions, this underrepresentation is less severe in family medicine given their call for concerted efforts to increase recruitment and retention of underrepresented groups. Research demonstrates that primary care clinicians, especially those who are underrepresented, are more likely to work in the underserved and marginalized communities already most affected by abortion bans, many of which are communities of color. A growing body of research indicates that racial/ethnic minorities have better overall experiences with clinicians who look like them, something that will be particularly important for patients fleeing abusive and unjust state laws.

To support increased abortion provision among primary care clinicians, we propose the following actions:

- Expand and fund abortion training in primary care to establish the necessary infrastructure (clinics, training sites, and residency programs) to train future clinicians, particularly in the border regions of less restricted states, such as southern Illinois, western Pennsylvania, western and eastern Maryland, and eastern Washington. States contemplating protections for abortion rights and clinicians should also invest in the renewal of this vital medical workforce.
- Remove institutional barriers that limit telemedicine, prescription of abortion medications, and elective training, as well as restrict licensure and malpractice insurance. We need to ensure that professional certifications, such as the new complex family planning subspecialty, includes non-ob-gyn physicians

and advanced practice clinicians, and that more restrictive states do not limit abortion provision to subspecialists.

- Implement policies to diversify and build the abortion care workforce in communities most affected by criminalization. This means expanding primary care with intentional efforts to increase recruitment, retention, and mentorship of people underrepresented in medicine. It also means collaborating with abortion funds and listening to and working with reproductive justice organizations. We must also seek out and hear the perspectives of people on the ground in restricted states.

We know the crisis of abortion access and reproductive injustice predates the fall of *Roe* by many decades, even centuries, and that it will take many more decades to address current and past harms. We must stand with broader human rights movements that include but are not limited to abortion rights. We must stand for the rights of all people, including ALL pregnant people. Ultimately, the expansion of primary care abortion provision is only one part of the broader coalition struggle that is needed to ensure that all pregnant people in the U.S. can access sexual and reproductive health care that is inclusive, equitable, and just.

About the Authors

Diana Carvajal is family physician and clinical health services researcher in the Department of Family and Community Medicine at the University of Maryland School of Medicine. She holds an M.D. is from the Rutgers Robert Woods Johnson Medical School and an M.P.H. from the Johns Hopkins Bloomberg School of Public Health. She serves as director of DEIA and Strategic Planning for RHEDI (Reproductive Health EDucation In Family Medicine).

Casandra Cashman is a family physician with a focus on sexual and reproductive health care and serves as director of program development for RHEDI. Her M.D. is from the University of Louisville School of Medicine.

Ian Lague is a medical educator and academic editor who serves as curriculum and program Manager for RHEDI.

GLOSSARY

abortifacient A drug or other chemical that induces an abortion.

amicus brief Advice or argument provided to a court by a person or organization that is not a party to the litigation the court is considering.

fundamentalism A belief that the literal meaning of a religion's sacred text should be the basis of morality and teaching.

gag rule A rule that prohibits people from speaking freely about a topic.

Griswold v. Connecticut A 1965 Supreme Court decision that affirmed married couples' freedom to buy and use contraception.

HIPAA The Health Insurance Portability and Accountability Act of 1996 protects health information from being shared without a patient's consent.

in vitro fertilization (IVF) Fertilization of an egg in a laboratory.

Medicaid A government program that pays for medical services for those unable to afford them.

telemedicine Medical care provided remotely to a patient using telephone, computer technology, or other digital device.

viability The ability of a fetus to live outside of the uterus.

FURTHER INFORMATION

Birgisson, Natalia E. et al, "Preventing Unintended Pregnancy: The Contraceptive CHOICE Project in Review," *Journal of Women's Health*, May 14, 2015, 349–353.

Dreweke, Joerg, "U.S. Abortion Rate Reaches Record Low amidst Looming Onslaught against Reproductive Health and Rights," *Guttmacher Policy Review* 20, 2017, 15–19.

Gold, Rachel Benson, "Lessons from Before Roe: Will Past Be Prologue?," *Guttmacher Policy Review*, March 2003, 8–11.

Heuser, Cara C., "What Quantum Mechanics Can Teach Us about Abortion," *Scientific American*, March 21, 2022, https://www.scientificamerican.com/article/what-quantum-mechanics-can-teach-us-about-abortion/.

Lenharo, Mariana, "These Drugs Could Restore a Period before Pregnancy Is Confirmed," *Scientific American*, October 26, 2022, https://www.scientificamerican.com/article/these-drugs-could-restore-a-period-before-pregnancy-is-confirmed/.

Maron, Dina Fine, "Abortions in Medical Settings Rarely Have Major Complications," *Scientific American*, December 9, 2014, https://www.scientificamerican.com/podcast/episode/abortions-in-medical-settings-rarely-have-major-complications/.

Mundy, Liza, "Pausing Fertility: What Will Happen When the Eggs Thaw?," *Scientific American*, May 1, 2019, https://www.scientificamerican.com/article/pausing-fertility-what-will-happen-when-the-eggs-thaw/.

Sole-Smith, Virginia, "Why Are Girls Getting Their Periods So Young?," *Scientific American*, May 1, 2019, https://www.scientificamerican.com/article/why-are-girls-getting-their-periods-so-young/.

CITATIONS

1.1 Lessons from before Abortion Was Legal by Rachel Benson Gold and Megan K. Donovan (September 1, 2017); 1.2 Abortion and Contraception in the Middle Age by Roland Betancourt (December 11, 2020); 1.3 Latin American Abortion Laws Hurt Health Care and the Economy–a Lesson for a Post-Roe U.S. by Emiliano Rodríguez Mega (January 4, 2022); 2.1 Many States That Restrict or Ban Abortion Don't Teach Kids about Sex and Pregnancy by Fionna M. D. Samuels (July 26, 2022); 2.2 Utah Kept Them from Learning about Consent, So These Teens Found a Place to Have 'the Talk' Together by Jesse Ryan (June 13, 2022); 2.3 Bioethics Faces a Virginity Test by Jacob M. Appel (March 2, 2020); 2.4 Yes, Phones Can Reveal if Someone Gets an Abortion by Sophie Bushwick (May 13, 2022); 3.1 Birth Control Pills Are Safe and Simple: Why Do They Require a Prescription? by Mariana Lenharo (June 20, 2022); 3.2 How Abortion Medications Differ from Plan B and Other Emergency Contraceptives by Tanya Lewis (July 1, 2022); 3.3 These Drugs Could Restore a Period before Pregnancy Is Confirmed by Mariana Lenharo (October 26, 2022); 3.4 Pregnancy Is Far More Dangerous Than Abortion by Adebayo Adesomo (May 30, 2022); 4.1 What Is the Point of a Period? By Virginia Sole-Smith (May 1, 2019); 4.2 Why Are Girls Getting Their Periods So Young? by Virginia Sole-Smith (May 1, 2019); 4.3 Pausing Fertility: What Will Happen When the Eggs Thaw? by Liza Mundy (May 1, 2019); 4.4 The Future of Sexual Reproduction By Karen Weintraub (March 1, 2018); 5.1 Abortion Pills Are Very Safe and Effective, yet Government Rules Still Hinder Access by Claudia Wallis (March 1, 2022); 5.2 Abortion Rights Are Good Health Care and Good Science by The Editors of Scientific American (May 5, 2022); 5.3 Being Denied an Abortion Has Lasting Impacts on Health and Finances by Mariana Lenharo (December 22, 2021); 5.4 To Prevent Women from Dying in Childbirth, First Stop Blaming Them by Monica R. McLemore and Valentina D'Efilippo (May 1, 2019); 5.5 Police Who Tear-Gas Abortion-Rights Protesters Could Induce Abortion by Matthew R. Francis (July 20, 2022); 6.1 Abortion Restrictions Could Cause an Ob-Gyn Brain Drain by Monique Brouillette (June 29, 2022); 6.2 Genetic Counselors Scramble Post-Roe to Provide Routine Pregnancy Services without Being Accused of a Crime by Laura Hercher (August 3, 2022); 6.3 Overturning Roe v. Wade Could Have Devastating Health and Financial Impacts, Landmark Study Showed by Tanya Lewis (May 3, 2022); 6.4 The Supreme Court's Abortion Ruling Upholds White Supremacy by Biftu Mengesha (November 1, 2022); 5.5 What the Supreme Court Should Know about Abortion Care by Cara C. Heuser (May 4, 2022); 7.1 Abortion Bans Based on So-Called "Science" Are Fraudulent by Nicole M. Baran, Gretchen Goldman, and Jane Zelikova (August 21, 2019); 7.2 How Abortion Misinformation and Disinformation Spread Online by Jenna Sherman (June 24, 2022); 7.3 Abortion Doesn't Have to Be an Either-Or Conversation by Amy Alspaugh, Linda S. Franck, Renée Mehra, Daniel Suárez-Baquero, Nikki Lanshaw, Toni Bond, and Monica R. McLemore (December 8, 2021); 7.4 Primary Care Providers Can Help Safeguard Abortion by Diana Carvajal, Casandra Cashman, and Ian Lague (June 24, 2022)

Each author biography was accurate at the time the article was originally published.

INDEX